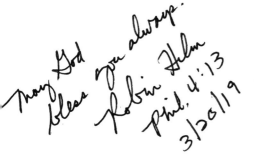

More to Love

My Beloved, My Friend: Book 1

ROBIN M. HELM

More to Love

By Robin Helm

ISBN-13: 978-1-79460-711-8

ISBN-10: 1-79460-711-0

Dedication

To Wendi Sotis, Laura Hile, and other writer friends who are my constant encouragers. To my readers who give me a reason to write.

Acknowledgments

I extend my heartfelt thanks to my editors: Gayle Mills, Wendi Sotis, Terri Davis, Laura Hile, and Larry Helm. My BeyondAusten.com readers also have my gratitude for reading this work as a work-in-progress and commenting.

Cover design: Damonza. [https://damonza.com/]
Formatting: Robin Helm and Wendi Sotis.
Cover model: Melanie F. Thompson
Cover photographer: Anna Beckham
Venue for cover photograph: Rosewood on Country Club Drive in Lancaster, South Carolina.

CHAPTER 1

But the Lord said to Samuel, 'Do not look at his appearance or at his physical stature, for I have refused him. For the Lord does not see as man sees; for man looks at the outward appearance, but the Lord looks at the heart.
I Samuel 16:7

Early October, 1811

The second eldest Bennet sister sat alone, trying to smile as she watched the couples dancing gracefully around the floor. Occasionally, she nibbled at the cookie she held, taking comfort in the richness of the sweet almond confection. As Elizabeth was a great favourite of Longbourn's housekeeper and pastry cook, Mrs. Bailey, she was never without several of the tasty morsels in her reticule. Mrs. Bailey, who had learned the recipes for several types of cookies while a young woman in America, kept Elizabeth well-supplied.

Knowing her mother would disapprove of her eating while she waited for an invitation to dance, Elizabeth practiced her usual ruse. She hid the jumble in her embroidered handkerchief, careful to let no one see it. In any case, she was rarely asked to dance, cookie or not, as there were always more ladies than gentlemen at Meryton's

Assemblies. This night had been no exception. She had danced only one set, and that with Joshua Lucas, a friend since childhood.

Her sister Jane's amiable partner for an earlier dance, Mr. Bingley, stood fairly close to Elizabeth, chatting with a handsome, austere man. Mr. Bingley's voice carried over the music and gaiety, impossible to ignore.

"Darcy! Why are you standing here with your arms folded when there are so many uncommonly pretty girls lacking dance partners? You should not keep yourself apart from the company in such a stupid manner when lovely young women are seated and gentlemen are scarce. 'Tis rudeness itself. I must have you dance."

"I certainly shall not," answered the gentleman, drawing himself up to his full, intimidating height, looking down his nose at his friend. "You have been dancing with the only handsome girl in the room, and your sisters are engaged at present."

Bingley's voice softened. "She is an angel, is she not? The most beautiful creature I ever beheld." He sighed. "However, there are plenty of suitable young ladies who are available."

Elizabeth smiled upon hearing his praise of her sister. Mr. Bingley's pleasant manner and good sense caused him to rise several notches in her estimation.

The young man continued, "Look! There is her sister, and she has a very pretty face, too. I daresay she is most agreeable. You must ask her to dance. Allow me to ask my partner to introduce you."

The young lady felt the weight of the gentleman's disapproving stare and glanced away, but she could not avoid hearing his reply.

"She is tolerable, I suppose, but there is rather too much of her to tempt me. Return to Miss Bennet and bask in her smiles, for you are wasting your time with me."

Elizabeth's eyes filled with unshed tears as she crushed the cookie hidden in her handkerchief. While she had never been obsessed with her looks in the way her younger sisters were, she always took pride in her appearance. Her father had often complimented her beautiful skin and her lustrous, thick hair, while her mother made certain her bonnets and dresses were stylish.

Even so, she grudgingly acknowledged to herself that she had been avoiding mirrors for at least two years now, and lately, her gowns had become uncomfortably snug.

True or not, his comments wounded her deeply. Though she was well-known for her intelligence and quick wit, she yearned to be told she was altogether lovely. She had many friends, but she feared that being bright and cheerful with a pretty face described a governess or a lady's companion, and she did not aspire to either of those vocations.

Secretly, Elizabeth wished to be the wife of a gentleman who adored her, as well as a mother to children she would love with all her considerable depth of heart, regardless of their outward features. She prided herself on valuing the characters of her friends and relatives rather than their physical attributes.

To be judged so harshly by a person she had never met was disconcerting. Her view of the world and her place in it was shaken.

In the moment the haughty gentleman had declared her to be "too much," she had become, to herself, "not enough." Not good enough. Not pretty enough. Not tempting enough.

Mr. Bingley, sweet man, would not agree with his friend. "How can you say that, Darcy? She has a perfect complexion, beautiful eyes, and dainty hands which are lovely. Her entire face is alight when she smiles, and I have also observed how graceful she is when she walks. Surely you have noticed that."

Darcy snorted. "I have. Who could miss it? She approaches the refreshment table every half hour, and she is sorely mistaken if she thinks her handkerchief hides what she is constantly eating. Bingley, I am not in humour to give consequence to young ladies who are slighted by other men, especially when that slighting is so obviously justified in this case by the lady's lack of discipline."

His companion rather testily replied, "I would not be as fastidious as you for a kingdom. You are determined to be disagreeable, so I will leave you to it. Furthermore, I shall dare your disapproval and ask her myself."

Elizabeth hardly ever allowed herself to dislike people to whom she had never been introduced, but she was willing to make an exception for tall, dark, brooding Mr. Darcy. Upon further reflection, she was somewhat surprised to realize she truly despised him, despite his arresting beauty and aristocratic profile. She had never formally met the gentleman, yet she could barely stand the sight of him. Odd, for she was generally accepting of everyone.

Seeing Mr. Bingley approaching her, she stuffed the handkerchief into her reticule and placed it under her chair. Her determined attempt at a pleasant countenance was successful.

A moment later, Mr. Bingley appeared before her, bowed, and extended his hand with a smile and a request.

Elizabeth stood and placed her hand in his, determined not to disgrace herself. She held her head high and fixed a smile upon her face, allowing her brilliant, green eyes to sparkle with mischief as he escorted her past Mr. Darcy onto the dance floor.

As she and Mr. Bingley moved through the steps, she glimpsed Mr. Darcy watching them several times, his dark eyes fixed upon her, an inscrutable expression on his striking face.
Assuming that he looked at her only to find fault, her active mind formed a scheme, and she could hardly wait to set it in motion.

Elizabeth awoke early the following morning, waiting for her sister Jane to stir.

Despite the fact that she had been abed only a few hours, Jane rose at her usual time and dressed quickly.

Elizabeth sat up, yawning, stretching her arms over her head. "Jane, why do you leave the bed so early every morning?"

The elder sister raised a brow. "I walk at least two miles, dear. Did I waken you?"

"No. I was waiting for you." She groaned. "Why must you do that at sunrise when you could sleep an extra hour and walk later?"

"The exercise is invigorating, and it wakes me quickly." Jane smiled sweetly. "I feel better all day if I take my constitutional before breaking my fast."

Elizabeth left the warm bed, shivering as she reached for her dress. "How long do you amble about?"

Jane chuckled as she quickly braided her long, blond hair. "I rarely amble. I prefer a brisk pace for an hour. Do you wish to join me today?" She wrapped the braids around her head and secured them.

"An hour?" Her eyes rounded. "A brisk pace for an hour? Before sunrise?" She gasped in shock. "In the dark? Alone?"

Jane buttoned the back of Elizabeth's dress. "It isn't really dark, Lizzy. 'Tis the best time of day. I love to see the sun come up from Oakham Mount. The countryside is beautiful when bathed in the light of dawn. I enjoy walking alone, but I should be glad of *your* company."

Elizabeth's expression was grim as she shoved her feet into her walking boots, quickly brushed her hair, and stuffed her curls up in her bonnet. After shrugging her arms into her rather tight pelisse, she faced Jane, her mouth set in a stern line. "If I can bear it, I intend to walk with you every morning from now on."

"In the afternoon, as well?" Jane slipped into her cloak and tied her bonnet beneath her chin.

Elizabeth raised both eyebrows. "You walk twice a day?"

Jane nodded. "In all weathers. You are usually reading or napping."

Elizabeth struck a dramatic pose, hand over her heart.

"I am done napping, and reading must wait until evening. I shall walk with you every time you go, through rain or sleet or hail or snow." She pointed towards the door. "Forward, ho!"

Jane laughed and clasped her sister's hand, pulling her from the room. "Come then. Time is wasting."

The sun was just beginning to peek over the trees as they arrived at Oakham Mount.

Jane breathed deeply of the chilly air. "Is it not lovely?"

"What?" asked Elizabeth, bent over with her hands on her knees, panting. Several long, chocolate curls had escaped her bonnet, and she pushed them back from her face.

"Why, the sunrise, Lizzy! Was it not worth leaving your bed to see this glorious sight?"

Elizabeth stood, clasping her hands to her middle. "Ah. Why, yes. 'Tis truly wondrous."

"Are you well, my dear?" asked Jane with concern, looking at her sister with troubled eyes. "Perhaps you have walked too far this morning."

Elizabeth shook her head. "I am well. My stomach hurts a bit, but if I sit on that tree trunk for a few moments, I am certain it shall pass." She sat down rather heavily, taking deep breaths.

"Going downhill is much easier than climbing, you know." Jane walked to stand beside her, placing her hand on her sister's shoulder.

"Thank heavens," muttered Elizabeth.

"What did you say, dear?"

She forced herself to her feet. "'Tis heavenly here, but we must return to Longbourn if we are to be there in time for breakfast."

Jane smiled. "I would rather be here than eat."

"Is this why you occasionally miss meals?"

She nodded. "It is so peaceful here."

Elizabeth laughed as she jerked her bonnet from her head, brushing her waist-length hair back over her shoulders with her hands. "And not so peaceful at home. Be that as it may, our mother shall be upset if we are not there, and we will suffer her bad mood all day."

Her sister grimaced and turned towards Longbourn with a sigh.

After making themselves presentable, Elizabeth and Jane hurried to breakfast, arriving to take their seats along with the rest of the family.

Once everyone was served, Mrs. Bennet fixed her satisfied gaze on Jane.

"My dear, you are radiant this morning. I thought you would lie abed after dancing so much last night. Why, I do believe you had partners for all the dances. I noted that Mr. Bingley claimed you for the opening set, as well as the supper dance. Such a fine gentleman. Mr. Bennet, you know he introduced himself to me nearly as soon as the girls and I arrived. So fortuitous that you visited him before the Assembly."

Lydia's triumphant voice rang throughout the room. "Kitty and I danced every dance, too, and Mary none!"

Ignoring his youngest daughter, Mr. Bennet smiled at Jane, and then turned his attention to Elizabeth. "And did you dance with Mr. Bingley, my dear?"

Elizabeth nodded. "I did, though I sat through much of the evening. As usual, there were not enough gentlemen present to partner all the ladies. I should have taken a book."

Her mother frowned. "Mrs. Long told me that the arrogant man with Mr. Bingley flatly refused to stand up with you. Mr. Darcy! Such an unpleasant bore!" She narrowed her eyes. "Several people heard what she said and talked of it at length. Who is he to think himself so far above his company, even if he is the richest man in Derbyshire?"

Elizabeth set her fork on her plate and looked down. "He did snub me, though 'tis of little consequence as he spurned all of Meryton." She lifted her eyes to her father. "Mr. Darcy danced with no one, save Mr. Bingley's sisters."

"He slighted my Lizzy, did he?" Mr. Bennet knit his brow. "I suppose the very rich can afford to give offense wherever they go, though being so free with his comments shows a distinct lack of good taste and breeding on his part. As he will undoubtedly soon be gone, we need not care for his good opinion."

"Even if he should ask you in the future," said her mother sharply, "you should not accept him. He is the proudest, the most disagreeable man who ever was."

Elizabeth sipped her tea. "He shall not ask me, so there is little chance I shall ever have the opportunity to reject him."

Jane gently touched her arm. "I think he must be shy, Lizzy. Why else would he act in such a way?"

"You are very sweet, Jane, but he is not shy," answered Elizabeth, her colour rising. "I heard his exchange with Mr. Bingley. He said he supposed I was tolerable, but there was too much of me to tempt him."

Seeing their shocked expressions unnerved her, so she left the table quickly, nearly all of her breakfast left uneaten upon her plate.

CHAPTER 2

*Do not judge based on appearances; a rich heart may be under a
poor coat.*
Scottish proverb

Darcy awoke at his normal time, despite the late evening before.
Sims, the gentleman's valet, accustomed to the habits of his master,
entered the room and opened the curtains, allowing the glow of
sunrise to enter the bedchamber.

The gentleman sat up and swung his legs over the side of the
bed, rolling his broad shoulders and stretching.

Sims bowed slightly. "Quite a lovely morning, sir. Will you ride
as usual?"

"Yes, send a servant to the stables to saddle my horse. I shall
break my fast afterwards."

As Sims crossed the room and opened the door, motioning for a
footman, Darcy rose, stretched, and went to his dressing room. He
smiled when he saw his riding clothes laid over a chair.

"Is all to your liking, sir?" Sims asked from behind him.

"Yes. I shall return and change clothing before joining Bingley
for breakfast."

Sims nodded. "A bath will await you. Do you wish me to shave you before you ride?"

Darcy shook his head. "No, I want to leave immediately."

"Very good, sir."

In a few moments, the gentleman was hurrying down the stairs, eager for his ride.

A young groom stood at the foot of Netherfield's steps, nervously holding the reins of Xanthos, Darcy's magnificent golden stallion.

The horse stamped in impatience as Darcy took the reins and swung himself into the saddle. He leaned to pat the stallion's neck, speaking softly. "Easy, boy. You are restless this morning. We shall ride until you tire."

He turned the horse with ease and galloped down the drive, heading into the fields without breaking stride. Xanthos left the path to climb an incline, and Darcy gave him his head.

Horse and rider paused at the top of Oakham Mount. As Darcy admired the glorious shades of the sunrise over the tops of the trees, a flash of colour caught his attention. He urged Xanthus forward until he could discern the forms of two young ladies nearly running down the slope.

To his utter amazement, he recognized Miss Jane Bennet's slender figure, but he stared a moment more before he decided the slightly shorter woman was her sister Elizabeth.

Miss Elizabeth's red bonnet was in her hand, and her long brown curls were loose, cascading down her back, catching the rays of the early morning sun.

The gentleman could not look away. She was wholly free and unspoiled, while he was rigid, confined by the rules of society. Her playful spirit, so different from his, fascinated him.

Remembering what he had said of Elizabeth the evening before, he shook his head. He knew himself to be an utter fool, as well as a liar. In fact, many of his friends preferred a lady's figure to be more rounded, rather than thin and angular. Several gentlemen in his set married ladies who had been slim when young, only to gain a bit as they aged. None of the men complained – quite the contrary. As he beheld her, completely unguarded, he fully agreed with them.

She was perfection.

Darcy had watched her as she danced with Bingley. She moved fluidly, laughing and chatting amiably with those around her. She was easy in company, while he stood alone.

Had he truly thought there was "too much" of her to tempt him? Too much of what, pray tell?

Grace? Beauty? Intelligence? Flawless skin and lively, expressive eyes? Good humour?

His musings provided him with a sudden, blinding insight into his own character. Perhaps he was the one who had "too much." Much too high an opinion of himself.

Darcy began to be uncomfortable with the direction of his mental wanderings.

He suddenly realized she had smiled at everyone else there – guests, musicians, servants, even a stray tabby cat – but not at him. He had been unable to look away as she danced with his friend and other partners for the remainder of the evening, but her expression turned to stone each time her eyes met his.

As they had never been introduced, there was only one plausible reason for her to glare at him.

Darcy groaned aloud.

She must have overheard what he said to Bingley.

While Elizabeth Bennet was certainly unsuitable for any liaison with the Darcy family, she did not deserve his disapprobation. He must have hurt her, and for that, he was truly sorry.

As she disappeared into the trees, he wondered, *What sort of man would wound the spirit of a woodland fairy?*

Darcy entered the breakfast room and sat to the right of his host.

Bingley's sisters, Caroline and Louisa, along with Mr. Hurst, Louisa's husband, arrived soon after.

A footman held Caroline's chair as she sat beside Darcy. Louisa and Mr. Hurst sat across from them.

Once they had served themselves, Caroline looked at her sister with a sneer.

"Did you notice the Bennet clan last evening?"

Louisa pursed her lips and sniffed. "Who could help but notice them? They were everywhere one looked. There was simply no getting away from them."

Caroline nodded, lifting a disdainful brow. "The mother is a shrew, the two youngest sisters are man-mad, and Elizabeth Bennet, who I have heard referred to as a famous local beauty, inhaled everything in sight. I will grant you that Jane Bennet is pretty and somewhat cultured."

She shifted her attention to Darcy." What say you, Mr. Darcy? Do you not agree?"

"Miss Bennet is quite lovely, but she smiles too much," he replied quietly, keeping his dark gaze on his plate.

"I will not have it!" exclaimed Bingley. "I will brook no criticism of Miss Bennet. She is the loveliest woman I ever beheld."

Caroline shook her head and waved a bony hand. "I agree that she is beautiful, but her family! Her father was too indolent to make an appearance last night, and the remainder of the Bennet family provided entertainment for the entire room."

She leaned forward and continued in her nasal tone. "I heard that Jane Bennet has an uncle in trade – in Cheapside, no less."

"Our father was in trade," interjected Bingley. "Miss Bennet is no less pleasant in my sight for having an uncle in Cheapside. I would still admire her had she uncles in trade enough to fill all London."

"Your father worked his whole life so you could be a gentleman," said Darcy firmly.

Bingley's voice was soft. "And is she not a gentleman's daughter? Mr. Bennet is a country gentleman with a small estate, but it is his and has been in his family for generations. I did not inherit any land; I must purchase it. How am I better than Mr. Bennet?"

Caroline nearly spewed her tea all over the table. She swallowed with difficulty and looked down her aristocratic nose at her brother. "You are far wealthier than the Bennets, and you are received in London society. Can you say the same for the Bennets?"

Darcy shifted uneasily in his chair.

Bingley tilted his head, glancing from Darcy to his sister. "I am received only because Darcy is my friend. If he befriended Mr. Bennet, that gentleman would be welcomed, as well. I do not pretend to think I was accepted by society on my own merits, for I know I am *nouveau riche*. I have no shame concerning what I am."

Caroline was not to be gainsaid. "Mr. Darcy, do you think Miss Bennett is a suitable match for my brother?"

"I believe she is lovely, kind, and all that is befitting a country gentleman's daughter," he replied.

"Yes, we all know that. There is no dispute on those facts," she said. "My question is, do you think Charles would do well to secure her hand?"

Darcy sighed, placed his fork on his plate, and stood. "If your brother marries her, he may materially damage *your* chances of making an advantageous marriage. It may not be right, but that is the way of the world."

He saw Caroline's smug expression before he left the room, and Elizabeth's face appeared in his mind, her long curls flowing freely about her shoulders.

The gentleman smiled as he walked away, thinking Caroline was no better a match for him than was Elizabeth Bennet, and in many ways that he now realized were quite important to him, she was far worse.

After an unremarkable day, aside from Mr. Darcy's rather enjoyable morning, the Netherfield party presented themselves at the home of Sir William Lucas.

Darcy stood apart from the crowd, observing the various occupants of the room with a stoic mien which belied his interest.

Again, Miss Elizabeth Bennet smiled and was merry with her friends, though never loudly enough to draw attention to herself.

No matter, as she had his full scrutiny without attempting to secure it.

However, Miss Charlotte Lucas, Miss Elizabeth's particular friend, seemed determined to put her forward.

"My dear Elizabeth, we must have a song. Will you not play and sing for us?" she asked.

Darcy listened with great attentiveness, hoping she would favour the request.

Elizabeth demurred. "You would have me perform in front of those who are in the habit of hearing the very best of musicians. I shall be censured, for I will certainly fall far short of the excellence they require."

Charlotte persisted, and eventually Elizabeth was swayed.

She glanced at Darcy, seeming to address him directly. "Very well. If you insist, I suppose it must be so, though I fear I shall be a grave disappointment to the company."

She took her place at the instrument and began to perform a pleasant song, greatly appealing to her audience.

Darcy's attention was wholly fixed on her when he sensed movement behind him. He glanced over his shoulder to see who approached him.

Caroline Bingley's mouth was much too close to his ear, and he shifted to his other foot, further away from her.

"I can guess the subject of your reverie," she said.

Her attempt at intimacy caused him further discomfort.

"I should imagine not," he answered in a clipped voice.

She lowered her voice to a whisper. "You must be considering how tiring it would be to spend many evenings in such a manner. The society is so far from genteel as to be annoying. I confess I am in total agreement with you. The cacophony that passes for music, the self-importance of the company, the insipidity! I should like to hear your opinion."

He leaned further away. "Your conjecture is completely wrong. My thoughts are more agreeably occupied in meditating upon the very great pleasure which a pair of fine eyes in the face of a pretty woman can bestow."

Caroline stepped up beside him, placing her hand on his arm, looking up into his eyes. "You must tell me who has inspired such reflections."

Darcy mustered every ounce of civility he possessed to stop himself from shaking her hand from his arm.

His answer was terse. "Miss Elizabeth Bennet."

"Miss Elizabeth Bennet! How long have you favoured large women? Upon my word, I thought the piano bench would crumble beneath her."

His manners stretched to the breaking point, Darcy turned to face her, dislodging her fingers with his movement. "And yet, I observe her lovely face and intelligent eyes."

Caroline raised her eyebrows. "I see she is a favourite with you. Pray, when am I to wish you joy?"

"You show little originality with that question. 'Tis exactly the response I expected. I knew you would be wishing me joy." He looked back at Elizabeth, surprised to see that she and Miss Lucas were observing the exchange.

"I consider the matter absolutely settled. You will have a charming mother-in-law, and, of course, she will be in constant attendance at Pemberley with you." Caroline laughed.

Darcy assumed his mask of indifference, but Caroline was undeterred. Her wit flowed long, and every word she spoke made him favour Elizabeth more and her less.

ROBIN HELM

CHAPTER 3

Outside show is a poor substitute for inner worth.

Aesop

Elizabeth awakened to the sounds of Jane dressing herself. She groaned as she forced herself to leave their warm bed and hurried to exchange her nightgown for a dress.

"Ah. I feared you would not wish to join me this morning," Jane said, smiling at her as she braided her long, blonde hair. "'Tis quite chilly, but we shall be warm soon enough if we walk rapidly."

Elizabeth silently pulled her dress over her head, and Jane stepped behind her to button it.

"It is unlike you to be so quiet, Lizzy." Jane began to brush her sister's hair. "Are you tired from staying up so late last night? Perhaps you should remain home today."

"I am a bit fatigued, but I will feel better after our walk."

"We walked twice yesterday, my dear. Are you not a little uncomfortable? You seem unusually quiet, and I heard the noise you made when you left the bed."

Elizabeth winced as she pulled on her pelisse and stuffed her hair under her bonnet. "I am a bit sore. I expected that I would be, so 'tis of little matter. Get your cloak. Hurry for I wish to see the sunrise again."

Jane bit her lip as she complied, and soon they were tiptoeing down the stairs.

Though she was winded by the time they reached the top of Oakham Mount, Elizabeth stood tall, hands on her hips as she stood facing the sun, willing herself not to pant.

"Why do you not sit for a moment, Lizzy?" asked Jane.

"You do not sit," answered Elizabeth, not looking at her sister.

"You shall not sit because I do not?" Jane placed her hand on her sister's shoulder. "You must tell me what you mean."

The silence stretched for several seconds before she answered. "I shall do what you do."

Jane angled her head. "You ate almost nothing all day yesterday."

"I shall eat what you eat and no more."

She gently put her hands on her sister's shoulders and turned Elizabeth to face her. "And why is that?"

Elizabeth jerked her bonnet from her head and threw it to the ground, following its progress with her eyes. "I am too heavy. Your figure is more pleasing. I wish to look like you."

"What?" Her sister's mouth dropped open in surprise. "Whatever put such a foolish notion into your head?"

"Not 'whatever.' Whoever."

Jane drew her brows together. "Has someone insulted you? I cannot imagine it. We are all friends here. Everyone loves you, Lizzy."

"Obviously not. Your Mr. Bingley pressed Mr. Darcy to dance with me at the Assembly."

"He is not 'my Mr. Bingley.'"

Elizabeth raised her head to smile at her sister. "I think he is; or he very soon will be."

Jane shook her head. "So, Mr. Bingley urged Mr. Darcy to dance with you. I suppose he refused. Since he danced with no one except Mr. Bingley's sister, I am not surprised the gentleman declined. Perhaps he feels awkward in company."

Elizabeth's bitter laugh cut through the chilly air. "He did not simply cry off, Jane. Mr. Darcy said there was too much of me to tempt him. He mentioned how much I ate."

Jane's eyes were knowing. "And Mr. Bingley danced with you himself."

"He did. He took pity on me after Mr. Darcy insulted me."

"This is not like you. You are attaching far too much importance to one man's opinion, Lizzy. He cared little for any of us. Why should you be so dismayed?"

Tears trickled down Elizabeth's cheeks, and she wiped them away angrily. "'Twas not only Mr. Darcy's judgment. I overheard Caroline Bingley talking to Mr. Darcy last evening at Lucas Lodge. She called me a 'large' woman and voiced her fear that the piano bench would not hold my weight."

"Surely you misunderstood her. It was quite crowded and noisy."

Elizabeth shook her head. "Charlotte heard her, as well. She then proceeded to denigrate our mother and wish Mr. Darcy joy. It was humiliating beyond belief."

"That makes no sense at all. Why would she wish him well?" asked Jane, frowning.

"For some odd reason, he defended me. Miss Bingley would not have that. Her next ploy was to intimate that Mr. Darcy and I would marry. 'Twas all a great joke with her."

"He defended you? How strange. What did he say?"

"He said I have a lovely face and fine eyes," she answered, blushing.

Jane drew her sister into an embrace, her voice gentle as she said, "He likely had not observed you very much when he spoke at the Assembly. When he saw you more closely at the Lucases, he changed his earlier judgment. That must have made you feel better."

"He said that simply to disagree with her," replied Elizabeth, pulling back, shaking her head. "It seems that Miss Bingley is set on having the very wealthy, infuriatingly handsome, dark-haired Mr. Darcy for her husband, and he is equally determined that she shall not be his wife."

"It is all most unsettling; however, I shall not have you starving yourself to spite people so wholly unconnected with us."

"Jane, you are my dearest friend. I am very far from starvation, and I ask that you help me rather than discourage me. What Mr. Darcy said is true, and I have known it for quite a while now. There is too much of me for my gowns to fit properly, and I will not ask for new ones. Papa is already concerned enough about the estate not doing well. Come. Let us return to the house. 'Tis nearly time to break our fast. You would not have me miss a meal, would you?"

Elizabeth picked up her bonnet and dusted it off. She slung it over her arm by the ribbons and held out her hand.

Jane laughed and took her sister's hand in hers. Together they ran down the hill, giggling like children.

As they reached the bottom, Elizabeth turned to look one last time at the sun peeking over Oakham Mount. She thought she saw a tall man on horseback, but she squinted, for the sun was in her eyes. When she shaded her brow with her hands for a better view, he was gone.

Mid-November, 1811

"Are you putting more food on your plate in an attempt to have me eat more, Jane?" Elizabeth whispered. "You cannot trick me. I will still eat only what you eat. I shall not be hoodwinked."

"Of what are you whispering, Lizzy? You know I do not allow such rudeness at my table." Mrs. Bennet proclaimed, delicately lifting her cup to her mouth and peering over its rim at her daughter in disapproval. "You must share your conversation with all of us."

"'Tis nothing, Mama," she answered, returning her attention to her breakfast.

Mr. Bennet rattled his newspaper, looking over it at Elizabeth.

Mrs. Bailey bustled in, waving a letter. "This note just come for Miss Bennet."

Jane reached for it, but her mother spoke quickly. "Give it to me."

With an apologetic look at Jane, the servant did as she was told. She turned to leave the room, glancing at Elizabeth's plate. The woman frowned, her kindly face uncharacteristically marred by the expression as she hurried from the room.

Mrs. Bennet broke the seal and unfolded the letter, reading rapidly. "Ah, Jane! You have been invited to dine with Mr. Bingley's sisters."

"Today? But it looks like rain," answered Jane, looking out the window.

Mr. Bennet folded his paper and placed it beside his plate. "I shall send for the carriage, my dear. I will not chance your falling ill."

"The carriage requires two horses, Mr. Bennet, and one of them is needed on the farm. Jane can go on horseback." Mrs. Bennet's voice was firm.

Jane shook her head. "I shall decline the invitation, instead."

Her mother narrowed her eyes. "You shall not. Daisy is well-able to take you to Netherfield. If you leave now, you will arrive before the rain begins. Should it continue to rain, you can stay the night."

Jane's distress was evident.

"Mama," implored Elizabeth, "Please, you must allow me to go with Jane."

"There is no need for that. You were not included in the invitation, and it would be rude for you to arrive with your sister. Besides, you cannot both ride Daisy. She cannot bear the weight of both of you together."

Elizabeth feared she could not hold back her tears, so she quietly stood and left the table.

Before she could get to her chamber, she felt a warm hand on her shoulder.

"What troubles you, child?"

She turned to face the owner of that beloved voice. "Mrs. Bailey. Come with me to my room."

Once they were in the bedchamber with the door shut, Elizabeth walked into the embrace of the woman who always comforted her.

The tall woman hugged her close, resting her chin on Elizabeth's head, patting the young lady's back as she sobbed. "Shh, now. Tell me why you cry, and I will give you the cookies I baked for you to make you feel better. You have failed to come to me this last fortnight at least for your favorite sweets."

She moved to hold Elizabeth at arm's length, hands on Elizabeth's shoulders, peering into her face.

"You must tell me, my little Lizzy."

"I – am – not – little," she sobbed. "I – am – huge!"

"What? Who has put that ugly thought into your pretty head?"

Elizabeth took a few deep breaths to calm herself. "I have heard people talking, and just now, Mama said Daisy could not carry both Jane and me."

Mrs. Bailey shook her head, clucking her tongue. "Mrs. Bennet is right, sweet girl. Daisy is old. She can hardly bear the burden of one of you girls, much less two. Your mother did not slight you. She loves you dearly. Now who are these 'people,' and what did they say?"

"Mr. Darcy and Miss Bingley both referred to my bulk."

"The new folks at Netherfield? I heard their servants refer to them as overweening. Why would you care what such people think?"

"You are right," answered Elizabeth. "I should not care, but I do."

"Is this why you have stopped eating? Why you do not come for your cookies anymore?"

Elizabeth dropped her eyes to the floor and nodded.

"I have seen you walking with your sister. I suppose we have Mr. Darcy and Miss Bingley to thank for that, as well." Mrs. Bailey tut-tutted. "I cannot believe you have set your world on end because of two haughty visitors to the neighbourhood. You are stronger than this."

"'Tis not only that. My gowns are too tight, and I can see for myself that my waist has thickened." She backed up and lifted her sad face to Mrs. Bailey. "I sit through most of the Assemblies now. The gentlemen dance with everyone else before they ask me. I refuse to be relegated to the wall flowers at twenty."

Mrs. Bailey raised a brow. "But would you want a man who disregarded you before you lost weight? One who did not value you for yourself but for how you look? I was once a beauty, you know. We all change. We all get older. Will such a shallow man turn away when you are no longer young and beautiful?"

"Again, you make perfect sense, but the man I marry will age with me. Beauty is not all a sensible gentleman requires, you know." She stood up straighter. "I am valuable in other ways."

The housekeeper smiled. "Indeed, you are. Now, are you still decided on your course?"

"I am."

"Then I shall help you. After your mother gives me the menus for the day, I will make certain to include plenty of fruits and vegetables, as well as leaner meats and chicken. I have a lovely recipe for roast chicken with egg sauce, though I shall serve yours without the sauce. I must suggest it to Mrs. Bennet."

"Excellent. Now, what about the cookies? I cannot resist them much longer."

Mrs. Bailey's blue eyes twinkled. "I'll not make your favourites again until you tell me to do so."

Elizabeth chuckled. "Wonderful! I fear I am not strong when your cookies are involved."

Mrs. Bailey patted her arm. "Neither am I. Perhaps we shall do this together. Misery loves company, or so I heard."

"Mayhap 'tis why Mr. Darcy and Miss Bingley are such great friends."

They laughed together as they quit the room, each intent on succeeding in their joint endeavour, making plans as they walked.

CHAPTER 4

First appearance deceives many.
Ovid

Darcy, Bingley, and Mr. Hurst left Netherfield on horseback an hour before they were to dine with the officers of the militia quartered in Meryton. Darcy had suggested they leave early, for he hoped to stop by the book shop prior to meeting the other members of their party. Bingley's library was sadly lacking, and he had requested Darcy's help in alleviating the problem.

After riding in silence for some time, reflecting on his good fortune in escaping Caroline Bingley for the day, the gentleman from Derbyshire looked up at the sky with a frown. "Did you observe the lightning in the distance? We must hurry. That sky promises more than light rain, and I have no desire to be caught out in a storm." He leaned forward to pat his horse's neck. "Xanthos heartily dislikes loud noises, and he becomes a bit skittish at the sound of thunder close by."

"Should we turn back?" asked Bingley, glancing at the golden stallion with trepidation. "'Tis beginning to look more and more like a thunderstorm approaches. I have rarely experienced such darkness at this time of day."

Darcy shook his head. "We are now much closer to Meryton than we are to Netherfield. I say we continue on our way at a faster pace. Perhaps the storm will pass over while we eat."

"If not, I can send for the carriage."

Darcy nodded and Hurst grunted in agreement.

The men urged their horses to gallop just as the first raindrops began to fall, splattering on their hats and coats.

Within a quarter hour, their horses had been stabled, and the gentlemen themselves were sitting at a table in the inn, waiting for the officers to arrive. The innkeeper's wife had taken their greatcoats, draping them over chairs in front of the fire to speed their drying.

Darcy passed the time watching the rain pound against the windows and splash in the street. A horse walked into his view, and he noticed a lady leaned over the animal's neck, her face turned away, her arms dangling loosely on either side. She seemed to be unconscious, unable to keep her seat. Concerned for her safety, he dashed through the door and ran to catch her.

The young woman slid from the horse just as the gentleman reached for her, but he was able to secure her against his chest. He staggered backwards, thinking he would at least cushion her if he was unable to keep his balance, but their fall was halted by strong hands supporting his shoulders.

Bingley shouted from behind him. "Give her to me! We must get her inside quickly."

Darcy turned with her still in his arms. "Take her, then." Her safety was his primary goal, and though he saw no advantage to her in honouring his friend's command, he was not so foolish as to argue in the street.

As soon as she was secure in Bingley's grasp and headed for the inn, Darcy grabbed the reins of her horse and led the mare to the stables.

By the time he returned to the inn, Darcy was drenched through, feeling chilled to his bones, his dark curls plastered to his head.

Bingley met him at the door. "I sent for my carriage and hired the inn's coach. We shall return to Netherfield as soon possible." He was clearly agitated.

Darcy crossed the room to stand before the wide fireplace, removing his jacket and throwing it over the chair with his greatcoat. Bingley joined him.

"Is it not a good plan?"

"Yes. I think we must return immediately. However, there are but three of us. Why have you engaged a second conveyance?"

"For Miss Bennet, of course. She cannot ride with three men. The innkeeper's wife has agreed to send her daughter with us; she shall return with the coach."

Darcy raised his brows. "Miss Bennet? The lady is Miss Bennet? I did not see her face. Why not send her to home to Longbourn?"

The set of Bingley's mouth betrayed his stubbornness on the matter. "'Tis closer to Netherfield than it is to Longbourn. Besides, she was on her way to Netherfield when she was caught in the storm."

"Why was she going to Netherfield?" *And how do you know that?*

Bingley's voice took on a tinge of anger. "My sisters told me this morning they had invited her to dine today because we were already engaged to meet the officers. The two of them admitted they wished to further a friendship with Miss Bennett but not create an opportunity for me to see her. I think they may have thought to gain more information concerning her family connections in order to discourage my attentions to her. In any case, they sent the invitation this morning, knowing full-well that rain threatened. I feel responsible for her situation."

How devious. "You may feel that way, but she has come to no harm. She is merely wet; she shall be dry soon enough. Miss Bennet is extremely healthy. She looks delicate, but she is no fragile flower. The lady walks in the morning and evening."

Bingley narrowed his eyes. "She walks in the morning and evening? I have no knowledge of her habits regarding exercise, so I fail to see how you learned such a thing."

Darcy bit his lower lip, realizing he had betrayed himself. "I ride every morning and evening, and I have seen her walking with her sister."

"Odd that she has never mentioned seeing you. Odder still that you never mentioned seeing her nor invited me to accompany you." Bingley tilted his head. "I talk with her every time we are in company together, yet she has not spoken of you at all."

"I doubt she ever saw me, though Miss Elizabeth may have," he said, shifting his eyes to the fire.

"How very strange that you never told me," replied Bingley softly. "I know you have no regard for Miss Elizabeth, so I must wonder if you are attracted to Miss Bennet." He paused. "I carried her up to her room, you know. She never left my arms until I laid her on the bed, cold and shivering."

"I fail to see your point."

Bingley smiled. "You compromised her by catching her as she fell from her horse, but your actions might be construed as heroic. I took her from you on purpose, bringing her into a roomful of people and carrying her up to a private room with only the innkeeper's wife as a nod to decorum. It appears that I have compromised her as well, but I was more thorough than you, and I have witnesses. You shall not take her from me, no matter that you are wealthier and better situated."

"Have you taken leave of your senses?" Darcy kept a firm rein on his temper, trying to remember that Bingley was one of his closest friends. "I have hardly spoken to the lady, and I had no idea who she was when I rescued her. There was no dark plan to claim her as mine. I could not marry her even if I wished to do so. You know that."

"You defended her against Caroline and Louise. You said that she was lovely and kind. I distinctly remember your remarking to me that she was the handsomest girl in the room at the Assembly. Did you tell me that she was unsuitable for me only to take her for yourself?"

Darcy sneezed violently. "I am unwell and unwilling to continue this conversation. You have my full support in pursuing the lady. Whether or not Caroline marries well is entirely up to you and your sister. Perhaps her fortune will secure her a match with an impoverished nobleman. There are plenty of those in our circle. I have nothing further to say on the matter."

"So, I have your approval?" asked Bingley.

"Do you need my approval?"

"No, but I should like to have it, all the same." He hung his head. "I am most sorry I accused you of being underhanded. You have always been a good friend to me, and I should not like to lose your friendship."

Darcy placed a hand on his friend's shoulder. "It appears you are a man in love, so you are forgiven your foray into unfounded jealousy. Perhaps you should make an offer to the lady, rather than depend on charges of compromise to win her. 'Tis likely she would rather have some say in the matter of her marriage." The gentleman punctuated his speech with another sneeze followed by a shiver.

The younger man looked at him with apprehension. "You are indeed ill. I shall have the local physician meet us at Netherfield. He can see you and Miss Bennet in the same visit, and I shall be able to apply that in bolstering my case for taking her to Netherfield."

Darcy looked at him askance. "I am delighted to be useful to your machinations. How fortuitous that I am cold and miserable. However, before you announce to the village and the inhabitants of Longbourn and Netherfield that I am sick, please allow the man to make that determination. Perhaps you should direct him to come here to see Miss Bennet and me."

Bingley looked at his feet. "I thought of that, of course, but I decided against it."

"May I ask why?"

The young man looked up, shame marring his expression. "He may not allow me to take her to Netherfield should he determine she is too ill to be moved."

Darcy shook his head. "Do you hear yourself?"

"I know I am selfish, but you must admit she will receive better care at Netherfield than she would here in a public inn with no one to attend her but the innkeeper's wife. I am thinking of her as much as I am thinking of myself."

"I rather doubt that."

"You must know I would never do anything I thought would truly endanger her," replied Bingley, looking earnestly at his friend.

"Then you will ask the physician to come here and take his advice concerning moving her to Netherfield?"

Bingley frowned. "I will. He shall be fetched posthaste. But know this, if Miss Bennet stays here, so will I."

"Then I shall remain here as well," Darcy replied with a sigh. "That way, you will be with me, and her reputation, as well as yours, shall be protected."

Bingley turned and strode to the innkeeper, who immediately called a boy and sent him scurrying out the door.

Before half an hour had passed, the physician, Mr. Jones, had examined both his patients and approved the plan to move them to Netherfield with instructions to go to bed and stay there until he arrived.

"I should much rather go to Longbourn, Mr. Jones. I have no wish to be a burden to the ladies of Netherfield," said Jane weakly.

"Nonsense, my dear," replied the kindly man. "Mr. Bingley insists that you must go with his party to Netherfield, for he knows you would not wish to spread the contagion to more than one house."

"More than one house?" she asked, alarmed. "Am I not the only one who is ill?"

"No, Miss Bennet," he answered, patting her hand. "Mr. Darcy is very much indisposed, as well. Would you have me run between Longbourn and Netherfield for the next week when I might visit only Netherfield? You know, Netherfield is much closer to my home than is Longbourn."

She drew her brows together, coughing into a handkerchief. "When you put it that way, I suppose I must go to Netherfield. I only hope I shan't make Mr. Bingley's sisters sick."

"Mr. Bingley thought you might say that, sweet child, and he was adamant that there would be no danger to anyone at Netherfield. He assured me he would send a letter ahead of the carriages, directing his sisters to stay in their rooms when you arrive. They will not be exposed to you or Mr. Darcy."

Though Darcy truly felt very poorly, he took upon himself the burden of writing a note to Mr. Bennet, apprising him of the situation. He knew the man would be unable to read Mr. Bingley's blot-covered scribbling and told his friend as much. Therefore, he spared Mr. Bingley the embarrassment of Mr. Bennet coming to Netherfield himself, having been unable to make heads or tails of his abysmal penmanship.

Bingley instead busied himself with sending instructions to Caroline, confident that she would understand his hand.

Servants hurried to outfit each carriage with blankets and warmers enough to please all the travelers, as well as the doctor. Once the rain had abated and the patients were comfortably settled, without further delay, the party began their journey to Netherfield.

ROBIN HELM

CHAPTER 5

Beauty is in the eye of the gazer.
Charlotte Brontë, Jane Eyre

Elizabeth rose from her bed before the sun breached the hills, determined upon her course.

A stable boy from Netherfield had appeared the prior evening with a note informing the inhabitants of Longbourn that Jane was quite ill and would remain with her hosts for the foreseeable future.

She had promptly announced in no uncertain terms to her parents that she would go to her sister, and would have left then, but her father forbade her to leave Longbourn so late at night.

Looking out her window, she muttered to herself. "'Tis no longer dark. I shall see for myself if my sister is suffering due to the manipulations of our mother. I know Jane would wish me to be with her, and nothing will stop my going."

The young woman dressed quickly, pushed her curls beneath her bonnet, and quietly crept downstairs, determined to make her escape before her family stirred.

"Good morning, my dear." Mrs. Bailey, holding a hamper, smiled at her from the foot of the stairs. "I thought you might try to slip past me."

Elizabeth chuckled. "Never. You know me too well. I was, however, attempting to depart before my parents and sisters could harangue me further." She paused and tilted her head. "What do you have in that hamper?"

"I packed a breakfast for you, as well as two packages of treats: one for you and dear Jane, and another for your hosts. You must not arrive empty-handed. Food equals love and sympathy where I came from. A gift of food shows good manners."

Elizabeth kissed her cheek and took the hamper by its handle. "You are very sweet. I know Jane will appreciate your thoughtfulness, and if the Bingleys and Mr. Darcy do not, I feel certain I shall be able to find someone who will. Everyone knows you are the best cook in Hertfordshire."

Mrs. Bailey patted her arm. "Now get along with you. Your father will soon be downstairs, and he may not allow you to walk three miles in the mud."

The young woman nodded as she walked towards the entrance, Mrs. Bailey following close behind her to open the door. She stood and watched Elizabeth until her favourite turned to wave at her from the crest of the hill, the first light of sunrise silhouetting her figure.

"'I think it an excellent thing I walk with Jane twice a day," Elizabeth said to herself. "Otherwise, carrying this hamper so far would surely have been too much for me."

She carefully hefted the bulky hamper over a fence, setting it on the ground before climbing over herself. Jumping to the ground, she was unaware that the back of her dress had caught on a rough spot. A ripping sound soon alerted her to the disaster. She looked behind her to assess the damage.

"No …" she groaned aloud. The bottom of her dress was torn and dirty.

However, Netherfield was in view. Her mood darkened further, and she spoke with vehemence. "'Tis too late to return home. I shall try to get in without being announced, unobserved by the superior sisters and dour Mr. Darcy."

She bit her lip in vexation. *Why am I always at my worst whenever I see that hateful man? He is always perfectly dressed and coiffed, and I am red-faced, sweaty, dirty, and disheveled. And out of breath.*

Elizabeth allowed her thoughts to go no further. Instead, she squared her shoulders, picked up the hamper, and marched across the grounds of Netherfield.

"I am determined to avoid the man in my present state," she said under her breath, looking at the ground as she hurried along. "I shall not give him further reason to despise me."

As she neared the house, she shivered, feeling she was being watched. Looking up quickly, she thought she saw a movement from a second story window, but before she could be sure, the curtain settled into place.

I shall go through the servants' entrance. Perhaps I could wash a bit of the dirt from my person before I see Mr. Bingley – or any of the other inhabitants of this grand house.

But it was not to be.

Mr. Bingley strode from the house, approached her, and took her burden. Silently, he led her to the front entrance where a servant stood by the open door.

The footman reached for the hamper as Mr. Bingley looked toward Elizabeth. "Where shall he put your basket, Miss Elizabeth?"

She blushed, thinking of facing the judgmental trio of Mr. Darcy, Miss Bingley, and Mrs. Hurst in her present state. "To my sister's room, please. I am come to inquire after her, and I shall follow him to her chamber."

"You may go, Sims. Give the hamper to Lily, who waits outside Miss Bennet's door. Tell her to put it in the lady's room. I shall escort Miss Elizabeth to see her sister after she breaks her fast." Bingley took her arm and began to guide her to the small dining room.

Elizabeth shook her head and came to a full stop. "I beg you, Mr. Bingley. I much prefer to go to Jane's room now. I would not appear at your table in such disarray. It would be an insult to you, your sisters, and your guest."

"I am alone this morning, Miss Elizabeth, and your appearance does not bother me in the least. In fact, I would be glad of your company."

She suddenly realized that Mr. Bingley, though kind as he always was, was unhappy. He did not smile. He was not his usual cheerful self, and she felt quite vain and selfish to be concerned with her appearance while he, quite obviously, suffered. She was mortified, for in focusing her attention on herself, she had failed to notice his distress.

But, why is he so upset? Jane must be very ill, indeed.

"Mr. Bingley?" she asked in alarm. "How is my sister? Is she in danger?"

He shook his head and looked away. "She is sleeping now. As you no doubt heard, Lily stays outside her chamber. She checks on Miss Bennet every half hour and reports to me. Mr. Jones has already been to see her this morning, and, upon his advice, I sent for my physician from London. Nothing further can be done for her or anyone else until Mr. Beckett arrives."

Elizabeth placed her hand on his arm. "It seems you have thought of everything. Since Jane is asleep, certainly, I shall eat with you, though I fear the dirt of my travel shall stain your carpets," she said softly, pointing to her muddy boots and the hem of her dress.

"The dirt?" He stopped and looked at her. "I had not noticed."

The gentleman motioned to a footman. "Take a basin of hot water to the retiring room. Miss Bennet also requires several towels. You must clean her boots as well as you can, and have a maid come back with you to assist her."

The young man nodded and hurried away.

Within a few moments, Elizabeth was washing her hands and face in the basin, handing the soiled cloths to the maid. She removed her shoes, leaving them outside the door, and pulled her bonnet off, leaving it on a table with the intention of retrieving it later.

When the maid attempted to brush her hair, Elizabeth waved her away, unwilling to spend so much time on her appearance before she went to Jane. Instead she ran her fingers through her curls, trying and failing to restore some semblance of order. Throwing her hands up in the air, she left her hair loose, flowing down her back.

I can do nothing further about my hair or this dress. Grooming shall simply have to wait. Let them judge me as they will.

After Elizabeth finished her attempt to make herself presentable and retrieved her boots, the maid showed her to the small dining room.

Mr. Bingley awaited her, standing by the sideboard. "Shall we serve ourselves?"

She joined him, and they quickly filled their plates.

Once they were seated, an uncomfortable silence filled the space.

"Where are your sisters and Mr. Darcy?" she asked, turning to her companion. "Have they gone to London to avoid the danger of contracting Jane's illness?"

"No, Miss Elizabeth," he answered gently. "Darcy is not doing well. He ran out into the storm to catch your sister as she fell from her horse. It appears he is in grave danger, and he is keeping to his rooms. My sisters were up quite late last night, as they were most distressed, and they have not yet come downstairs."

The guilt of her uncharitable thoughts stabbed her as tears filled her eyes. She turned her face away, reflecting on how wrong she had been.

Mr. Darcy risked his own health to help my sister. He cannot be as bad as I thought.

She dropped her gaze to her clasped hands. "I am most sorry. I had no idea he was ill. I wish there was a way I could help him."

"You must stay here, then. I shall send to Longbourn for your clothes, as well as Miss Bennet's, directly. Miss Bennet will be much better if you are with her, and you may be able to read to Mr.

Darcy. Caroline would gladly do it, but I fear she would hover, and he would hate that."

Elizabeth quickly returned her attention to the gentleman. "I thank you for your thoughtfulness, Mr. Bingley, and I should be happy to be with my sister, but I am wary of sitting with Mr. Darcy in his chambers. Would that not be highly improper? Would he approve of such a plan?" she asked, hoping for a negative answer, for it seemed far too intimate for her comfort. "Can you not read to him?"

"I tried last night, but he soon asked me to stop," he replied, shaking his head. "Normally, I do not read for entertainment. Therefore, I have not his relish for reading poetry and classic literature, and I fear I cannot do his favourites justice. However, he has mentioned you to me several times, praising your taste in music and literature. A maid and I can sit with you. Whatever you require to put you at ease will be done."

Mr. Darcy has praised me? I do not believe it.

"Sir, you are surely mistaken. To my knowledge, he has heard me play but once, and he can have no knowledge of my taste in books. We have had no conversation beyond a sentence or two."

Mr. Bingley looked at her solemnly. "Perhaps he overheard you talking with someone else. I shall ask him if he should like for you to read to him. If he wants you to do it, will you agree? A few footmen can carry him to the small drawing room adjoining his bedchamber and place him on a couch, if that would make you more comfortable. You could even leave the door to the hallway open."

Elizabeth strove to keep her voice low and persuasive. "Why are you so insistent on this matter? I shall be busy enough with Jane."

He drew his brows together and sighed. "When you see Miss Bennet, you will expose yourself to the illness she and Darcy suffer. I have already been with both invalids, but I insist that my sisters stay away from them. We must limit the number of people who could possibly contract whatever sickness they have. Mr. Jones was adamant on the matter. You and I, along with a few servants, must care for your sister and my friend in order to stop the spread of the contagion. Both of them sleep a great deal. I think you could read to Darcy while she sleeps."

She took a deep breath, affected by his pleas for assistance. "I concede that you may be correct. However, you must ask him while I listen at his chamber door. I shall be guided by what he says. We should ask the physician if moving him is safe. I would not wish to repay his kindness to my poor sister by putting him in further distress, and one room is really no different from another if you and a maid are with me."

"Excellent," he replied, smiling for the first time since she had arrived. "I shall send for your things and hers immediately. If you go to your sister now, she may be awake. You can change into a clean gown when your trunk arrives, then I shall talk to Darcy while you listen. Agreed?"

She was resigned. "Agreed." She hesitated a moment. "I shall write a note to my father and include a list of my favourite books to be brought from Longbourn."

"A wonderful notion! My own library is in a sad state. Now, Mills will show you to your sister's room," Bingley answered, gesturing to one of the footmen.

Elizabeth followed the man, deep in thought.

What have I agreed to? Why could I not think of an excuse? I feel certain Mr. Darcy dislikes me as much as I despise him.

She shook her head, remembering that he had helped her sister at his own expense.

Why would he risk his own health for a person he deemed so wholly beneath him?

ROBIN HELM

CHAPTER 6

*Men in general judge more from appearances than from reality. All
men have eyes, but few have the gift of penetration.*
Niccolo Machiavelli

Darcy felt his head would surely explode. He would have held it
together with his hands, but his attention was diverted by the
realization that his entire body was on fire. Chills and fever had
plagued him, alternating throughout the night and day, and he ached
in every muscle.

The gentleman from Derbyshire was normally a taciturn man,
unwilling to speak unless he was compelled to do so, but now, only
the greatest inducement would cause him to impart his thoughts. He
desired nothing so much as solitude and darkness, for light greatly
increased his suffering.

Yet, Bingley had ordered the curtains drawn and stood before
him, looking for all the world as if he desired to converse.

Darcy closed his eyes, hoping against hope his friend would
think him asleep and leave him be.

"Darcy. Are you awake? Darcy, I must talk to you."

Confound it all. He pried his eyes open. "I am now. What do
you want?" he croaked, his throat hurting with the effort.

He thought Bingley glanced towards the door, but he could not
be certain of it.

41

Darcy attempted to lift his head and see if anyone else was in the room, but his stiff neck and shoulders would not permit it.

Bingley held a glass of water. "Are you thirsty?"

The gentleman nodded, and his friend held the glass to his lips. When Darcy was finished, Bingley set the empty glass on the table by the bed.

"Darcy, I have a question to ask." Bingley hesitated, looking towards the door again.

Is someone at the door? "Is Beckett here?"

Bingley shook his head. "No, but he should arrive very soon. In the meantime, shall I read to you? I know you must be ready to run amok from boredom."

"You woke me to ask if I would have you read aloud? Nothing in your library is worth reading," Darcy growled, coughing deeply. He put his hand over his chest and rubbed the soreness.

Listening to Bingley's reading is terrible enough. Listening while Bingley reads drivel is even worse.

He had an earache, along with pain in every fiber of his being. The damp sheets stuck to his body; he badly needed a bath, along with a change of his bed linen. Darcy was decidedly unhappy.

"I – sent for more books – ones you would like."

Darcy sighed. "Bingley, I have no wish to injure you, but there is no book in the known world which would not be ruined by your reading style," he said hoarsely.

Bingley's face fell. "I know, but I think I have a solution."

The gentleman raised a brow. *Please, please, I beg of you. Do not suggest Caroline read to me. I am suffering enough already.*

"What if someone else read to you instead? Someone who enjoys the same books you like." Bingley's voice was wheedling.

Darcy groaned. *'Tis like kicking a puppy. I already feel bad enough without this.* "No one here reads anything that would interest me."

"Miss Elizabeth Bennet does."

"Miss Elizabeth Bennet is here?" *Probably to see her sister.*

The gentleman brightened in spite of himself. He very nearly assumed a pleasant expression. Fortunately, his head pounded at that moment, reminding him that he was most definitely not going to smile.

Bingley grinned. "Indeed, and she sent for a crate full of her favourite books. She will stay to care for Miss Bennet, but I feel sure she would also read to you, if you wished for her to do so."

I would be at a distinct disadvantage. I must look positively horrible, and I cannot allow her or anyone else to see me looking like this. He drew a deep breath. *Bingley has a fresh scent, but I smell like an animal – a pig comes to mind. Perhaps a goat. A wet dog?*

"She would not wish to spend her time with me, Bingley, for she is here for Miss Bennet." *I would not wish to raise her expectations, even though I admire her. I never toy with a lady's affections.*

"But what if she agreed to entertain you with a book you would enjoy? She could read a passage, and you could discuss it with her. I am astounded at how much she knows. No other woman of my acquaintance is as well-read or as intelligent as Miss Elizabeth."

Bingley began to rub his lower lip with his index finger, his face a study in deep thought, obviously considering a conundrum.

He seemed to reach a conclusion. "However, upon second thought, you may be right. You would be quite humiliated should you not be able to keep up with her lively mind. Please accept my apologies. I should never have brought it up." Bingley waved a well-manicured hand and turned to go. "I shall leave you to your rest."

Darcy drew his brows together and painfully cleared his throat, coughing again. "Bingley."

The younger gentleman looked back. "Yes?"

"Are you sure the lady is willing? Should we risk her succumbing to my illness?"

Bingley returned to Darcy's bedside. "She has already exposed herself by tending to her sister."

"I should not want to take her from Miss Bennet, especially if the lady feels as poorly as I do." *Though no one else could possibly feel as poorly as I do. Indeed, they would be dead.*

"Miss Elizabeth would come to you only when her sister sleeps."

Perhaps it might cheer me a bit, but what would people say? "Would she not worry about gossip? I should not like to ruin the good reputation of a superior woman."

Thinking he heard a gasp from the hallway, Darcy again tried, and failed, to raise his head enough to see the door.

Bingley grabbed an extra pillow and tucked it under his friend's head, helping him to sit up a bit.

"Did you hear something just outside the door?" asked Darcy.

Bingley leaned over him, displaying his concern by placing his hand on Darcy's fevered, though noble, brow. "Are you hearing things? Having hallucinations?" He straightened up and wrung his hands. "Where could Beckett be? He should be here by now!" Bingley looked wildly around the room.

Darcy turned his eyes heavenward. "Calm yourself. It must have been a footman."

Nodding energetically, Bingley replied, "I am certain you are right, as you usually are."

Darcy watched the door suspiciously. "Was that a muffled chuckle?"

"Shall I look in the hallway?"

The gentleman frowned. *Perhaps I am imagining things. Can Bedlam be far behind?* "No, I think not."

"Have you decided to agree to having Miss Elizabeth read to you? I can stay with her, along with a maid, to protect her innocence."

Darcy glared at him. "Her innocence? She is in no danger of being despoiled by me."

"I completely understand. You are no threat to young ladies. The very idea is preposterous."

He coughed. "What can you mean? I am much a threat as any other gentleman when a beautiful lady is alone with me. Are you questioning my manhood?"

Bingley bit his lip. "Oh, I would never do that. I know you are quite dangerous. I think I shall tell Miss Elizabeth that you fear you cannot control yourself with her, and she should avoid you at all costs."

"Who is laughing in the hallway?" he attempted to bellow. It was not impressive, as he wheezed in the middle of his rant. "That is no footman. 'Tis a woman's voice."

"Perhaps I should go see who is there. The maid may be waiting with your morning repast. I shall have to dismiss her without a reference if she laughed at you."

"No. Stay. A maid would have no reason to be merry at my expense. She must have exchanged a joke with a footman. I would not have her turned out for being cheerful." He huffed a bit. "And I am quite able to manage my impulses. Please tell Miss Elizabeth that I should sincerely appreciate it if she would read to me at her convenience."

"As you wish. A maid and I will stay in the room. I would very much enjoy hearing the young lady read a novel or poetry. When you are well enough, we can move you to a chaise lounge in your sitting room."

"If you insist. Where is Roberts? He must have some hot water sent up. I need to bathe before I see anyone."

Bingley sniffed, wrinkling his nose. "A capital idea. I am certain a soak in the tub will make you – *feel* better."

Darcy narrowed his eyes. "I beg your pardon. I have had no opportunity to wash since yesterday morn, as I have been quite occupied in being ill."

"And you are most fastidious. I understand," replied Bingley in a soothing tone. "Since I told Roberts to leave you in my care, I shall go give him your instructions and speak to the housekeeper concerning food and drink for you and Miss Bennet."

Darcy closed his eyes, exhausted by the conversation. "Tell him to wake me when the bath is ready. I am fit to see neither man nor beast, and certainly not Miss Elizabeth, in my present state."

Bingley's shoulders shook as he headed towards the door. He made an odd, choking sound.

He is behaving quite strangely this morning. Is he falling ill as well? I shall ask Beckett to see to him.

Darcy's thoughts drifted as he fell into a light slumber, dreaming of a lovely, dark-haired young gentlewoman. Her voice was low and melodic while she read to him. It was a delightful dream, and he clung to it as long as he could.

As he regained consciousness, he felt a hand on his shoulder. All that remained of his dream when he opened his eyes was a strange sense of disappointment, for there was Roberts, and the beauty was gone.

"Shall I help you to the bath, sir? I took the liberty of having the footmen move the tub to this chamber. You shan't have to walk so far, and a screen shields it from the rest of the room."

"Excellent, though I think I can walk that short distance alone," Darcy mumbled in reply. "Be sure to wash my hair."

"Sir? I thought you would want a very quick bath. You do not seem quite yourself."

Because Darcy was so dizzy he nearly fell when he attempted to stand, he allowed Roberts to assist him from his bed to the bathtub.

After his valet undressed him, Darcy reclined in the warm water, allowing his muscles to relax and his mind to wander.

"Are you ready to go back to bed, sir?"

"Have you asked for clean linen?"

"I shall ring for a maid," answered Roberts.

"Wait. Wash my hair and fetch a clean nightshirt and robe. I wish to be clothed when the maid comes in. I am not yet able to leave this room, but I think I am able to sit up while you arrange my hair."

"Very good, sir."

46

Roberts followed his instructions to the letter, and within an hour, Darcy was back in his bed, resting on fresh bedclothes, eating eggs and toast, drinking tea, and feeling a bit more like a man than a dog.

He was inordinately pleased to find that he smelled better, as well.

Satisfied that he was up to hearing a good book read properly, he looked forward to Miss Elizabeth's visit.

When Mr. Beckett and Mr. Jones arrived, however, Mr. Bingley escorted them straight to Darcy's room.

The gentleman's pleasure was to be postponed. For the second time in the space of two hours, he was most unhappy.

Mr. Jones stood aside as Mr. Beckett examined the patient.

Darcy was even more disgruntled as the physician poked and prodded him, listening to his chest, checking his heart, and peering down throat.

Finally, the man put away his instruments. "'Tis an excellent thing you have the constitution of a horse, Mr. Darcy. Otherwise, the situation would be dire."

"How so?" inquired the patient.

"You have influenza. London is presently suffering an epidemic, and many children, along with the elderly and sickly, have died from the disease. You will likely suffer a great deal in the next few days, but, no doubt, with proper rest and treatment, you will survive. Were you in London recently?"

Darcy nodded. "We came here from Town but a few days ago. I noticed many people were sick, yet they still came to soirees and musical evenings. I was ready to leave the place and come to the country. However, Miss Bennet was not in London. How did she contract the disease?"

"She was the only lady you favoured with a dance at the Assembly, apart from my sisters," replied Bingley, "and they wore long gloves."

"But I never touched Miss Bennet. She wore gloves, as well."

Bingley was somber. "Miss Bennet wore gloves most of the evening, but her sister, Miss Lydia, bumped into her, causing her to spill her punch. She removed her gloves before she danced with you because they were wet."

"I brought a plague upon the neighborhood." Darcy looked up at the ceiling. "What if she dies? I should not have come here."

"Nonsense," answered Mr. Beckett. "Someone else in the vicinity may have passed through London recently. There is no way of knowing why the lady became ill. Have you been around the people of the village since the Assembly?"

Bingley thought a moment. "We visited a local family, and we were in the village inn during a thunderstorm. Darcy caught Miss Bennet as she fell from a horse. They were both drenched."

"We may be fortunate, then. Perhaps the only two cases will be the young lady and you, Mr. Darcy. After I examine Miss Bennet, I shall give a treatment regimen to your housekeeper."

Bingley followed him. "I shall go with you, to show you the room, of course."

Darcy burrowed under the cover, his mood very low.

She shall not come to read to me once she knows 'tis my fault her sister is ill. She loves her sister dearly, and she will not forgive me.

CHAPTER 7

*Judge not that you be not judged. For with what judgment you judge,
you will be judged; and with the measure you use, it will be
measured back to you.*
Matthew 7:1-2

Elizabeth sat by her sister's bed, reading aloud from *The Ingenious Nobleman Sir Quixote of La Mancha* by Miguel de Cervantes.

Hearing her sister's even breathing, Elizabeth lapsed into silence.

Jane groaned, and Elizabeth rose to her feet, placing her hand on her sister's forehead and setting the book on a small bedside table.

She is far too hot. No wonder she is restless. I doubt she heard a word I read, and Don Quixote is one of her favourites.

Elizabeth dipped a cloth in the water basin on a table by the bed and gently sponged Jane's face. She looked up, leaving the cloth on Jane's forehead as Mr. Jones entered the room, followed closely by a golden-haired, handsome man who carried a satchel.

Mr. Jones nodded at her and glanced up at the tall, young gentleman. "Miss Elizabeth, allow me to introduce Mr. Thaddeus Beckett, Mr. Darcy's physician. He just arrived from London, and he is here to determine the extent of your sister's illness."

Mr. Beckett bowed gracefully while Elizabeth extended her hand, lowered her eyes, and curtseyed. He took her fingers lightly as he straightened to his full height and smiled at her.

The power of speech left her when her gaze travelled from his smile to his eyes. He had the most beautiful, light blue eyes she had ever beheld, and they were observing her with undisguised interest.

She quickly recovered, taking a deep breath as she pulled her hand from his grasp and stepped away from the bedside. *I shall not look at him again. I become a blithering idiot when I do.*

"My sister, Jane. Thank you for coming to see her," she said, gesturing towards the prone figure under the coverlet.

"Ah! I see you've been reading Cervantes," he said. "I read his short stories as a younger man. Now I greatly enjoy his poems and other works, as well, especially *Don Quixote*. I know very few ladies who enjoy his work."

Elizabeth focused her attention to his forehead, studiously avoiding the rest of his face. "I suppose you must count my sister and me among the bluestockings. *Don Quixote* is one of Jane's most beloved books."

He raised an eyebrow, drawing her eyes to his.

"But not yours?" he asked.

Again, she was caught by his blond good looks, and she quickly fixed her gaze on Jane.

I refuse to make a fool of myself over a man who very likely agrees with Mr. Darcy concerning my ample figure. She shook her head. *Even if Mr. Darcy did refer to me as 'beautiful,' I must remember the poor man was likely talking out of his head due to his illness.*

"I enjoy a multitude of authors and literary forms, but Alexander Pope challenges me. I like authors who make me think."

She was satisfied with her answer. *I am not a ninny.*

I may be a bit too frank, but I am known for my honesty. I will not change for a face which surely should belong to a Greek god. Apollo? The god of healing and medicine, light and truth. Perfect.

Mr. Jones cleared his throat rather loudly. "Perhaps you could look to Miss Bennet now, Mr. Beckett. Do you think she suffers the same malady which afflicts Mr. Darcy?"

"I would prefer to delay my examination until the lady is awake. I do not wish to startle Miss Bennet by touching her while she sleeps."

His voice was low and rich.

Musical. Apollo played a golden lyre.

Elizabeth mentally shook herself and leaned over her sister. "The physician is here from London," she whispered.

Jane's eyes fluttered open. "Lizzy? I am awake." She put a hand to her throat.

She looked at Mr. Beckett, and then back to Elizabeth. "Have I died, or am I dreaming?"

"Neither, dearest. Why would you ask that?" Elizabeth's brow creased in worry.

Jane pulled her down, speaking softly, her words intended for Elizabeth's ears only. "Is that an angel? Has he come to take me to heaven?"

Elizabeth blushed bright red and murmured her reply. "No, Jane. 'Tis Mr. Beckett, the physician come from London."

The patient sighed deeply and closed her eyes. When she opened them again, she was serene. "Mr. Beckett, thank you for coming," she said quietly in a rasping voice.

If the young man had heard the exchange, he had the good manners not to show it. "Miss Bennet, I fear you have the influenza, as Mr. Darcy does. Do I have your permission to examine you now?"

Jane nodded slightly, and Elizabeth stepped aside.

Mr. Beckett turned to Elizabeth. "Your sister seems to be confused. Please, go to the other side of the bed and hold her hand. Talk softly to her while I check her symptoms."

Elizabeth nodded and did as he requested.

When the physician was finished, he washed his hands in the basin on the washstand. "Miss Elizabeth and Mr. Jones, please join me just outside the door."

After directing the maid to sit with Jane, Elizabeth followed him, noting his broad shoulders and elegant posture.

He is as handsome from the back as he is from the front. I am a terrible person for looking at him in such a way, but how can I not notice?

The gentleman looked troubled. "Your sister does indeed have influenza, and I fear she will be worse before she is better. I am concerned for her lungs, but I also worry about her confusion. Has she eaten today?"

Elizabeth shook her head. "She complains with her throat each time I try to feed her."

"It is as I thought. I studied with Mr. Matthew Dobson, among others, a few years ago. He thinks people with a certain condition exhibit such symptoms when they go without food for too many hours. Forgive me, but I must ask, have you ever noticed a sweet smell from her chamber pot?"

Elizabeth widened her eyes, her colour deepening. "How odd that you should ask. I have remarked on it to Jane several times."

"It is as I thought. She has too much sugar in her blood and must eat regularly to make her brain work properly. The state of a person's physical body can cause damage to the mind. Mr. John Rollo, another colleague, published a recommended diet for such instances. I shall write it down for you. In the meantime, she must eat something sweet. 'Tis the fastest way to limit the glycosuria and stop her mental fog, though she should not make a habit of ingesting sugar. That would be detrimental to her health."

Her face brightened. "I have some sweets sent with me by our housekeeper at Longbourn. Jane was so ill, I entirely forgot about them."

She opened the door, hurried to the hamper, and returned with two wrapped bundles, untying the string from one of them as she walked back.

"What are those?" asked Mr. Beckett, his blue eyes sparkling. "They look delicious."

"Cookies," answered Elizabeth, handing him a jumble.

He took a bite and smiled. "Mmmm …. Wonderful! Sweeter than biscuits. Mr. Jones, help me to raise Miss Bennet to a sitting position. I dislike having to disturb her, but we have no choice. Miss Elizabeth, place pillows behind her to hold her up while she eats. Get a glass of water while I break the cookie into small pieces. She should drink water in between bites."

Elizabeth followed his instructions quickly and was rewarded by his frequent approving glances towards her.

Her stomach fluttered. *How odd. Perhaps I am ill, as well.*

Jane had greatly improved by the time they finished feeding her, and the gentlemen quit the room to find Mr. Bingley.

The master of Netherfield had been most adamant that they apprise him of Miss Bennet's condition as soon as Mr. Beckett finished his visit with her.

Elizabeth dressed for dinner early, allowing herself enough time to read to Mr. Darcy for an hour before the meal. When she was ready, she presented herself to Jane for approval.

"Shall I embarrass you, my dear?"

Jane smiled weakly. "You look quite lovely, Lizzy."

"Are you certain I should not stay and read to you instead? Mr. Darcy would not mind."

"I am quite tired. I shall sleep while you are gone, and you can bring my dinner and feed it to me when you return. You must amuse me by telling me everything that happens while you are away."

Elizabeth kissed her forehead. "Sarah will sit with you while I am absent. She will fetch anything you need. You must tell her, you know. Send her if you want me to come back. I shall be cross if you do not."

"I saw how you looked at Mr. Beckett. I think you like him, Lizzy."

"I confess I do like him. Indeed, I do not know how anyone would not like him."

Jane nodded. "He is quite handsome. Is he not?"

Elizabeth felt the blush rise from her neck to her cheeks. "Yes. Very handsome. He may be the handsomest man of my acquaintance. An Apollo come to life."

"Interesting. You have known him all of half an hour, yet you compare him to a mythical god."

Elizabeth chuckled. "Does he not look like a being who could harness four horses to his chariot and force the sun to move across the sky? He has every appearance of goodness."

Jane nodded slowly. "He does, but I am surprised you would decide his character based on his visage. As I recall, you objected most vehemently when a certain gentleman judged you in the same way."

Elizabeth was speechless for the second time in one afternoon. *She is right. Mr. Beckett looks angelic, but he may be a devil for all I know.*

"When did you become so wise?"

"I have been admired for my blond hair, blue eyes, and slender figure for many years now. However, no one ever thinks me intelligent or capable. I am seen as too kind, gullible, easygoing. I trust people until they prove me wrong, but I am not stupid. Do you understand?"

"And I am routinely thought of as intelligent, but not as pretty as you are."

Jane's smile was sad. "I would rather be thought of as wise than beautiful. Beauty fades rather quickly."

Elizabeth leaned down and gathered her sister in her arms. "You are both, my dearest one."

"You love me, so you think the best of me. Should you not extend the same latitude to someone you do not know so well? Mr. Darcy judged you based on your appearance, and he was wrong in that, but he risked his own health to save me from injury. I wish you would reconsider your low opinion of him."

"I will try, to please you."

Jane closed her eyes. "My throat feels raw. It hurts when I speak."

She looks so tired. Perhaps the nap will do her good. "I shall go then. You need to rest."

Elizabeth collected a book, along with the bundle of cookies for Mr. Bingley, and left Jane to the care of Sarah. She strode down the hall to Mr. Darcy's room with purpose, determined to do what Mr. Bingley had asked of her.

I also will consider what Jane said. I shall attempt to forget what he said about me and act without prejudice, as I would with any new acquaintance.

As she had arranged earlier, Mr. Bingley and Susan, a young maid, awaited her just outside the gentleman's chambers.

Elizabeth handed Mr. Bingley the packet of cookies. "My friend baked these for you. Jane and I enjoy her sweets very much."

He accepted her gift with a smile. "You came."

She raised a brow. "I told you I would. Is he awake?"

"Indeed. He refuses to sleep for fear he will miss your visit."

Elizabeth shook her head, pursing her lips. "I do not believe you for a minute. I prefer that you enter first; I shall follow you."

Mr. Bingley opened the door, directing Elizabeth to the chair by Mr. Darcy's bed. After placing the cookies on a table, he and Sarah sat nearby.

"Do you like Alexander Pope, Mr. Darcy?" asked Elizabeth. *He hardly looks ill. In fact, he is in remarkably good looks for a man at death's door.*

He nodded, dark eyes gleaming. "I do, Miss Bennet. How did you know?"

"He is one of my favourites, and I thought we might share an admiration of his work."

"I have often thought we would agree on many things, including, but not limited to, a similar taste in literature. What work did you bring to read to me?"

She showed him the cover. "I am fortunate to have Pope's complete works with me. Do you have a preference? *An Essay on Criticism*? *An Essay on Man*? His translation of *The Iliad*? I shall allow you to choose."

Darcy smiled, and her heart skipped a beat.

She took a deep breath. *I have never seen the man smile in such a way before. I hope he chooses the most pedestrian of Pope's works.*

It was not to be.

Darcy tilted his head, watching her. "*The Rape of the Lock.*"

"You jest, sir."

"Oh, no. I am perfectly serious."

She opened the book to the correct page and swallowed hard. *I should never have given him a choice. I am surely doomed.*

CHAPTER 8

*Charm is deceptive, and beauty is fleeting; but a woman who fears
the Lord is to be praised.*
Proverbs 31:30

Darcy awaited Elizabeth's visit with an excitement he refused to
acknowledge. His feelings would not bear close examination.

He was thankful to be ill, and he could not fathom it, for he had
never before embraced any perceived weakness in himself.

When she finally arrived, sat, and began to converse, he longed
to know her better. Given the choice of Pope's works, he decided to
surprise her by choosing an early poem written by the man.

"The Rape of the Lock."

Her face fell. "You jest, sir."

*You thought I would choose a long, serious essay which would
have predicated a deep discussion, and very likely, resulted in
further discord between us. I am in no mood for an argument with
you, Elizabeth.*

"Oh, no. I am perfectly serious," he replied, unable to stop
smiling.

"Very well."

She cleared her throat and began to read aloud.

What dire offence from am'rous causes springs,

What mighty contests rise from trivial things,
I sing — This verse to Caryl, Muse! is due:
This, ev'n Belinda may vouchsafe to view:
Slight is the subject, but not so the praise,
If She inspire, and He approve my lays.

Say what strange motive, Goddess! could compel
A well-bred Lord t' assault a gentle Belle?
O say what stranger cause, yet unexplor'd,
Could make a gentle Belle reject a Lord?
In tasks so bold, can little men engage,
And in soft bosoms dwells such mighty Rage?

Elizabeth glanced up at him, speculation written on her face. "Why did you choose this poem?"

"What did you think I would choose? A boring, academic work? Something very dry and pedantic? Like me?"

She narrowed her eyes. "I refuse to judge you based on so short an acquaintance and very little information."

He lifted his chin. *Even though I judged you unfairly. We shall deal with that.*

"You have never judged me? I thank you for your forbearance. You are a better person than I." His smile was innocent. "I will admit that I have, from time to time, made statements based on first impressions, and those too quickly-formed opinions are occasionally wrong."

"Only occasionally?" Elizabeth's skeptical expression was not lost on the gentleman from Derbyshire.

Mr. Bingley made a choking sound behind them.

"Water," he said in a strangled voice, waving a hand. "I need water."

Coughing, he rose and left the room.

"Shall I continue?" asked Elizabeth.

"By all means, please do."

"As you wish."

She read quickly, soon arriving near the end of Canto III.

> The Peer now spreads the glitt'ring Forfex wide,
> T' inclose the Lock; now joins it, to divide.
> Ev'n then, before the fatal engine clos'd,
> A wretched Sylph too fondly interpos'd;
> Fate urg'd the shears, and cut the Sylph in twain,
> (But airy substance soon unites again)
> The meeting points the sacred hair dissever
> From the fair head, forever, and forever!
>
> Then flash'd the living lightning from her eyes,
> And screams of horror rend th' affrighted skies.
> Not louder shrieks to pitying heav'n are cast,
> When husbands, or when lapdogs breathe their
> last;
> Or when rich China vessels fall'n from high,
> In glitt'ring dust and painted fragments lie!

Darcy chuckled, and Elizabeth stopped reading.

"You are amused?" she asked, smiling.

"You are not?"

"Of course, I am. I simply wonder if we are entertained by the same things. Why do you laugh?"

I laugh because you enchant me. You make me happy. There. I admitted it, he thought.

Darcy gave her the full force of his complete attention. "Pope has perfectly captured the falseness of society. The gentleman cut a lock of Belinda's hair to keep – a memento of the woman he loved. He did not hurt her or molest her in any way. He had no intention of offending her. It was improper, yes, as well as a liberty, but there was no harm done. Her hair would, after all, grow back rather quickly, yet she screamed as if he had stabbed her."

Her voice was soft. "I feel certain you know the poem is based on a true event. The families remained estranged. It was not trivial to her relations, for they viewed it as symbolic of a loss of chastity and virtue."

Darcy shook his head. "You are right, but I think Lord Petre would have married Miss Fermor. He was not a rake, and he made his admiration of her plain enough. However, she was a celebrated beauty who thought her looks were spoiled by his act."

"I admit it was a storm in a teacup," Elizabeth replied, "though he seemed to have recovered quickly. After all, he married a rich heiress a year later. I was sad, however, to learn that the gentleman died of smallpox a year after his marriage when he was but twenty-three years of age. He left his sixteen-year-old bride with child. A true tragedy. Do you not agree?"

He nodded solemnly. "I do. Arabella Fermor did not fare much better, for she allowed the notoriety of being the principal player in Pope's farce to puff her up. Vanity working on a weak head produces every sort of mischief. She was known as a troublesome and conceited lady after *The Rape of the Lock* was published. I have never envied her husband. She was, by all accounts, very lovely, but she could not have been an easy companion. Beauty does not last forever."

"And I have never had sympathy for the man," said Elizabeth firmly. "Mr. Perkins got what he wanted – a wealthy, beautiful, high society wife. I have often wondered if he was pleased with his lot. A London belle, she married him and retired to the country to escape the humiliation of Town after the scandal. She used him. I would not wish to be married under those circumstances."

The gentleman replied gently. "They both received what they wanted from marriage. That is the modern way, you know. Very few wealthy gentlemen or ladies marry for love."

"Would you?" Her voice was a whisper as she glanced behind her.

Darcy looked puzzled. "Would I marry for love?"

"Yes."

He raised his eyebrows. *I have not thought of it. Would I want a woman to marry me for my wealth or station in life but not love me? I do not think so.*

He shook his head. "I would not marry without it."

"But you require more."

Darcy observed the stubborn set of her jaw. *You will not like my answer, but I will always be truthful with you.*

"I have familial obligations which I cannot ignore." He frowned. *What an unusual conversation.* "What of you? Would you marry a poor man for love?"

She sighed. "I have no thoughts of matrimony at all, Mr. Darcy. I refuse to marry unless my groom and I mutually love one another. From what I have seen in the world, with the exception of my Aunt and Uncle Gardiner, there are very few love matches."

Elizabeth laughed. "Shall I make a good governess? Or perhaps a companion for an elderly lady? One widow might be easier to manage than six children."

You will choose a life of servitude rather than marry a man who could provide you with comfort? You laugh, but you know you will have almost nothing when your father dies. You must not refuse an offer that could provide for your welfare. Your spirit will die in such cold confinement.

And yet, his heart wrenched within him at the thought of her married to another man.

The door opened, and they both looked towards the sound.

Mr. Bingley entered, followed closely by Mr. Beckett.

Elizabeth closed the book and rose to her feet. "I must go as well. Jane asked not to be disturbed, for she wishes to sleep. Shall I see you both at dinner?"

"Most certainly," answered Mr. Bingley. "We came to fetch you and make sure Darcy has everything he requires."

I would rather she would eat with me, but I cannot detain her. Darcy stifled a yawn. "Perhaps you could bring me a tray after you dine, Bingley. I would like some tea for my throat."

"I shall send something up with your man while we eat, for Beckett and I hope to hear Miss Elizabeth perform tonight. My sisters and brother will join us for dinner; Caroline and Louisa have already agreed to play for the party. We shall visit you again afterward."

Elizabeth's smile faded. "I think I must return to Jane after we dine, Mr. Bingley. I would not wish to leave her alone for too long. Your sisters are quite able to entertain you and Mr. Beckett."

Darcy noticed Beckett's expression. *He seems to be disappointed. Did he look forward to an evening with Elizabeth?*

He had never thought of Beckett as anything other than his physician. Now he studied the man's face and figure. *He is certainly handsome in a way that ladies would appreciate, and he was born a gentleman, though a second son. Odd that he refused a commission in the military or a vocation in the Church, instead choosing to be a physician.*

The gentleman sighed. *Without a doubt, Bingley's sisters think he is worthy of their attentions. Otherwise, they would remain in their rooms.*

Darcy took comfort in the knowledge that Elizabeth would return to her sister's chambers following the meal.

She had the chance to spend the evening with Beckett, and she refused. He smirked.

The physician touched Elizabeth's arm. "Miss Elizabeth," he began earnestly, "I shall go with you to check on Miss Bennet after we dine. If she still sleeps soundly, will you agree to play for us? I have so looked forward to hearing you, for Bingley told me he has rarely heard anything else that pleased him so much."

Elizabeth blushed and turned her face up to his with a sweet smile. "I do not enjoy performing in company, sir, but since you have so kindly looked after my sister, I will play for you if she still sleeps when our meal is over. 'Tis the very least I can do, for you have asked nothing else of us."

Watching the scene play out, Darcy clenched his jaw.

The young physician held out his arm to her, and she accepted it.

As Mr. Beckett led her from the room, Mr. Bingley looked at Mr. Darcy and grinned.

"They make a lovely couple, do they not, Darcy?" he whispered before he followed them and closed the door. "He would be an excellent match for her."

Darcy glared at the ceiling. *Lovely, indeed. Perhaps she will not be in service after all. She will marry Beckett and have a dozen golden children, for he looks as if he loves her already. Why would he not?*

The thought should have made him happy, for he truly wished Elizabeth to be loved by a good man and well set up in life.

I admit I want to be the good man she loves. I want to take care of her and our children. Our dark-haired, dark-eyed children, playing on the grounds at Pemberley. I would teach my sons to fish and ride and my daughters to gather flowers for their mother. I would take them into Lambton to meet the townspeople, like my father did Georgiana and me. They would gather around Elizabeth and me as we read them stories. I could push them in the swing that hangs from that big oak tree.

He mourned the children he would never have with her as he turned his face to the wall. *Georgiana will marry and move away, and I will be alone.*

Though Darcy knew Elizabeth was unsuitable for him in every way that mattered to his family, he longed to feel the silk of her thick hair sliding through his fingers, to bask in the warmth of her smile, to see her green eyes flash, to learn what interested her, and to share her secrets.

"I love her," he whispered aloud, unable to suppress it any longer. "But I can never marry her."

ROBIN HELM

CHAPTER 9

You are altogether beautiful, my darling. There is no flaw in you.
Song of Solomon 4:7

Elizabeth sat across the table from Thaddeus Beckett, who was flanked on either side by Mr. Bingley's sisters. Mr. Hurst was to her right, and Mr. Bingley was at the head of the table to her left.

She found the arrangement very satisfying, as Mr. Hurst seldom spoke, preferring instead to drink and eat with great enthusiasm. Apart from answering the occasional question put to her by the other members of the party, she was at liberty to observe the scene unfolding before her.

Caroline Bingley was in fine form.

She leaned towards Mr. Beckett. "You have quite hidden yourself away, Mr. Beckett. I hope you will consider attending more social functions when you return to London. My brother knows many influential people. I am sure he would be happy to introduce you into Society, and if you attend a ball, I will make certain you have a partner for every dance."

I had no idea I could be shocked by Miss Bingley, but it seems I was in error. Elizabeth took a spoonful of soup. *She is positively predatory.*

Mr. Bingley cleared his throat. "Caroline, Beckett has no need of my sponsorship. He eschews Society only because he wishes to do so. In fact, he could move in better circles than ours, should he desire it."

Caroline's eyes were round as she turned to the physician. "Are you a member of the peerage, sir?"

"I am the second son of the Duke of Ormonde," he answered stiffly, placing his glass on the table.

"You are the mysterious Lord Thaddeus? Why do you not claim your heritage?" she asked.

"I do not wish to," he said. "I am a commoner by law and a physician by choice. My profession gives me the means to help people. I would rather live a meaningful life than a dissolute one. Too many young men of my acquaintance have wasted themselves in idleness and dissipation. My mother always taught me, 'Idle hands are the Devil's workshop.'"

The lady gaped for a moment before she recovered enough to assume her practiced smile once more.

She looks like a fish. Elizabeth chuckled quietly. *Jane would disapprove of my uncharitable thoughts.* She attempted to keep her face from showing her mirth, though she knew her eyes most likely betrayed her merriment.

"Surely you cannot mean that all men should work," said Miss Bingley. "If a gentleman is well established, why would he spend his time laboring? There are plenty of amusements available which are not decadent. My brother and Mr. Darcy do not engage in business."

Mr. Bingley leaned forward in his chair. "Caroline, you go too far."

Mr. Beckett smiled. "Do not distress yourself, Bingley." He shifted his attention to Miss Bingley. "Of course, they work. Darcy has the oversight of the Pemberley estate. He must be a man of business to assure that the land provides a living for his family as well as his tenant families. From what I have observed, he takes that responsibility quite seriously. Your brother is seeking to buy an estate, and I think he shall follow Darcy's example. If he does, he will have to work very hard indeed."

He looked back at Bingley. "Do you not agree, sir?"

"You know that I do. You have heard my conversations with Darcy in London. I assure you he has no admiration for men who do not view land ownership as a grave duty. The lives of so many people depend upon the successful running of the estate."

Elizabeth thought of her own situation. As her father and mother had produced no male heir, Longbourn would go to a cousin upon her father's death. Her choices were quite limited, for her father had not earned enough from the estate to provide for her, her four sisters, and their mother.

"I must say I admire your ethics, gentlemen," she said quietly. "Your concern for the tenants and families of an estate is commendable. I think you would be an excellent master, Mr. Beckett."

The gentleman looked her squarely in the eyes. "I hope I am."

"In the future?" asked Elizabeth.

He bit his lower lip for a moment. "No, now. I hope I am a good master presently."

Miss Bingley raised her eyebrows. "You already own an estate?"

Elizabeth lowered her eyes. *The hound has scented the fox. Run, Mr. Beckett!*

Mr. Beckett nodded. "It is not generally known, but I inherited an estate in Suffolk from my maternal grandmother. She felt that my elder brother was already adequately provided for, so she left her land, home, and fortune to me. If I were given a choice, I would rather my grandmother were still alive rather than have Beltham."

"How do you handle both the management of your estate and your profession at the same time?" asked Miss Bingley. "You must never have a spare moment."

Mr. Bingley shook his head. "Caroline! Have you not pried into Beckett's affairs enough already?"

Holding up a hand, Mr. Beckett replied, "Bingley, as I am the one who brought up my ownership of an estate, I have no problem answering your sister's questions."

He dropped his hand to his lap, shifting his blue gaze to Elizabeth. "I employ both an estate manager and a man of affairs, and I visit Beltham at least twice each month to inspect the books, as well as the property. Since my eldest sister is widowed, she and her children live there, and she handles the staff. As for my profession, I have a partner. When I am not in Town, he sees my patients if they are ill. I do the same for him when he is gone."

Miss Bingley looked from him to Elizabeth, her mouth set in a thin line. After a moment, she stared at her. "How is your sister, Miss Elizabeth? I am sure you are quite eager to return to Longbourn. You must miss your family exceedingly."

"I am enduring it as best I can, Miss Bingley. Thank you for your concern, but my sister is still too ill to be moved. I look to Mr. Jones and Mr. Beckett to tell me when she is well enough."

"Miss Elizabeth has four sisters, all unmarried, and the estate is entailed away upon a cousin. Is that not right, Miss Elizabeth?" Caroline Bingley looked triumphantly at her perceived rival.

Elizabeth closed her eyes for a moment. Before she opened them again, she attempted to assume an expression of serenity. "Yes, Miss Bingley. You are correct. When my father is dead, Mr. Collins may turn us out as soon as he pleases. We must depend upon God to provide for us."

Mr. Beckett regarded her with sympathy. "I understand your situation better than you know, Miss Elizabeth. My sister and four nieces live with me because her husband's estate was also entailed. The gentleman who inherited was a married man with a large family of his own, and he assumed ownership of the property immediately. My sister did not wish to return to my father's estate, and she had nowhere else to go, so I asked her to live at Beltham and help me by keeping the house running smoothly. A lady needs her own household to manage."

Caroline Bingley gasped, causing her to choke on a bite of roast chicken, and her brother's lips twitched as he gestured to a footman. "Fawcett, get help. My sister is in distress."

"Allow me," said the young physician, standing and using the side of his hand to strike her sharply between the shoulder blades.

The offending piece of fowl popped violently from the lady's mouth, flew across the table, and hit her indolent brother-in-law squarely in the forehead.

Mr. Hurst dropped his fork and looked up for the first time that evening. "Shall we have any sport tomorrow? Today was a tedious waste of time."

Several events occurred in quick succession.

Miss Bingley fled the room in tears.

Mrs. Hurst threw her napkin on the table and glared at her husband before she followed her sister, head held high.

Elizabeth stood, blurting, "I must see to Jane." She fairly ran for the door, her hand over her mouth.

"I shall come with you," said Mr. Beckett, pushing back his chair.

"And I will wait in the hallway," added Mr. Bingley, following closely behind them.

Mr. Hurst remained in his seat, calmly finishing both a bottle of wine and his dinner.

Later that night, Jane was sleeping soundly, so the two gentlemen went to Darcy's room, hoping to find him resting, as well.

Elizabeth was restless. She had missed her walk the previous evening, though she had managed to leave Netherfield before sunrise that morning, determined to have her exercise.

I need to tire myself out, or I shall get no rest this night. She quickly changed into her oldest dress, as well as her walking boots, before she donned her pelisse and bonnet.

After telling Sarah her plan, Elizabeth crept stealthily through the hallway, down the stairs, and out the front door. The sun had set hours before, but the moon was full, and she knew the way to

Oakham Mount as well as she knew her own name. Unafraid, she set out at a brisk pace.

As she continued deeper into the trees, she heard a twig snap behind her and looked back. *'Tis only a small animal. No one is there.*

Another sound, and she stopped to listen, turning slowly. *Footsteps. Something large.*

Her breathing increased. *Between me and Netherfield. I cannot go back.*

She bolted at full speed, hoping to find a place to hide, but her fear drove her forward. *I shall run all the way to Longbourn, if I must.*

Only a few steps into the open space surrounding Oakham Mount, she tripped and fell, sprawling on the ground, hitting the side of her head on a large rock.

Just before she fainted, Elizabeth thought she heard someone call her name from a great distance. *I know that voice.*

As she came back to herself, she opened her eyes and saw golden hair surrounded by a halo. "Are you an angel, come to take me to Heaven? Have I died?"

"Thank God!" replied the angel, kneeling next to her. "You are most certainly alive, Miss Elizabeth, though you gave me quite a scare."

She tried to sit up, but the strong angel stopped her, holding her by the shoulders as he leaned over her. *His face is in shadow. I want to see him.* She lifted her hand to touch his cheek. *There is stubble. Do angels have beards like mortal men?*

He untied her bonnet and carefully removed it from her head. *I am safe with him.*

She felt his fingers in her hair, lifting her head a bit, removing the pins and setting her curls free.

"Let me help you sit up slowly. I would not have you faint again, but I must check your head. You fell and bumped it."

"Who are you?" she asked.

She felt his hands moving gently across the back and sides of her head, stopping over a tender spot.

"Do you not remember me? I am Thaddeus Beckett, a physician. Fortunately, your bonnet and hair must have protected your head somewhat when you fell. You have quite a lump, but there is no blood." His voice was filled with relief.

"A physician? Not an angel?"

His laugh was low. Melodic. "I assure you that I am a flesh and blood man – not an apparition and most certainly not an angel."

He is glorious. "You are beautiful."

The man stopped and looked down at her. His voice was soft. "You are the most beautiful woman I have ever seen. You are the angel." He gathered her up in his arms, holding her as if she were a child.

Tears filled her eyes. "You speak of my sister, I think." Her voice broke. "You must put me down. I am far too heavy for you to carry."

"Where did you get such a preposterous idea? You are perfect."

Elizabeth shut her eyes, and the tears ran down her cheeks. "Mr. Darcy refused to dance with me. He said there was too much of me."

Mr. Beckett clenched his jaws, striding towards Netherfield with Elizabeth in his arms.

She put her head against his chest, listening to the steady beating of his heart, wanting nothing more than to sleep.

His deep voice rumbled against her cheek as he muttered, "The man is an idiot."

ROBIN HELM

CHAPTER 10

*Do not let your adornment be merely outward – arranging the hair,
wearing gold, or putting on fine apparel – rather let it be the hidden
person of the heart, with the incorruptible beauty of a gentle and
quiet spirit, which is very precious in the sight of God.*
I Peter 3:3-4

Darcy had hardly fallen asleep when he awoke to the sound of a
commotion outside his door. He tried to sit up, but his head pounded,
and he abandoned the effort. His chills returned, so he pulled the
covers closer, as he struggled to breathe. *I did entirely too much
today.*

The gentleman reached for the bell his valet had left by his bed
and rang it. He waited a few minutes and rang it again, with more
force.

Roberts opened the door and bustled into the room,
straightening his jacket as he walked. "Yes, Mr. Darcy? What may I
do to assist you?"

"I need some hot tea for my throat and something to ease this
pain in my head. Could you ask Beckett to prepare something for
me?"

Roberts bowed slightly. "I shall bring the hot tea immediately,
but Mr. Beckett is with the young lady just now. I will speak to him
as soon as he is free. I feel certain Mrs. Brooks kept his directions

for making a willow bark brew. I shall tell her to prepare it immediately."

Darcy raised his head with a frown. "Miss Bennet is worse? Was that the cause of the noise in the hallway just now?"

The valet shook his head. "Miss Bennet is as she was, but her sister fell and hit her head while out walking at Oakham Mount, and the whole house is in an uproar."

"Miss Elizabeth must be relatively well, or she would not have been able to walk back."

"Oh, she could not have come back on her own, sir, for she has been in a dead faint or out of her head since her accident, according to what I heard. I do know Mr. Beckett carried her into the house himself and refused to put her down until a room was prepared, for I saw that myself. She is just down the hall in the room beside her sister, and he has not yet left her side."

Darcy sat up in agitation, headache momentarily forgotten. "She must be badly injured, indeed." *Why was she at Oakham Mount in the middle of the night? How did Beckett come to be carrying her? Were they together? The scoundrel! Did she meet him willingly? Her reputation will be in tatters.*

He groaned and grabbed his head with both hands as the throbbing pain came back in full force. *I brought him here, thinking he was a man of honour. This is all my own doing, and so must the remedy be.*

"Who else is with Miss Elizabeth and Beckett?"

Roberts looked puzzled. "Why, Sarah, I suppose. Shall I find out for you, sir?"

If Caroline cared the least bit for propriety or what could be happening under her own roof, she would be in there with them. She has made it clear that she despises the Bennets, but does she not realize that her lack of caring for Miss Elizabeth could give rise to vicious gossip connected with Netherfield and her own family? And where is Bingley? The Bennet sisters are under his protection. Since he is nowhere to be found, I shall act in his stead.

74

Darcy swung his legs over the side of the bed. "I must speak to Beckett. As it appears he will not leave Miss Elizabeth, I shall go to him. Bring me my clothes and help me dress."

"Sir!" exclaimed the valet. "You can hardly walk, and you must not leave the room for fear of spreading the influenza."

"Both Miss Elizabeth and Beckett have already been exposed. Dress me at once."

His voice brooked no opposition, and Roberts rushed to do what he was told. Before a quarter hour had passed, Darcy was fully clothed and walking with his valet's assistance to Elizabeth's chambers.

As Roberts opened the door, Beckett stood and faced them.

Livid that he was alone with Elizabeth, Darcy fought to keep from raising his voice. "I must speak with you immediately."

Beckett raised an eyebrow. "Indeed? I fear our conversation shall have to wait, sir, for I cannot leave my patient alone. Someone must keep her from sleeping for several hours."

"Then Roberts and Sarah shall stay with her. You and I have business which cannot be delayed."

Beckett's gruff tone and narrowed eyes betrayed his anger. "Most certainly. I think we are in complete agreement on that, at least. Sarah should be back very soon. She just stepped out to fetch tea for Miss Elizabeth and me to help us stay awake."

Elizabeth's eyes were round as she looked between the two men. Her gaze settled on Darcy. "Who are you?"

All the air left his lungs. *She no longer knows me.* His heart seemed to twist in his chest.

Beckett leaned over, smiling at her. "This is Mr. Darcy. You know him rather well. Do you remember?"

She closed her eyes briefly. "Mr. Darcy? Why are you here? To disapprove of me again?"

Darcy's face reddened. "Again? I have never disapproved of you, Miss Elizabeth. I am here only to help you."

She looked up at Mr. Beckett with adoration. "This angel is caring for me. Is he not beautiful?"

Beckett is a beautiful angel, but somehow, I am the devil? He frowned. *This will not do at all.*

Sarah entered, bearing a tea tray, and Darcy glanced at Roberts. "You and Sarah shall make certain Miss Elizabeth does not sleep. Mr. Beckett will be back shortly."

He turned to the maid. "You are not to leave Mr. Beckett and Miss Elizabeth alone together again, and you shall not speak of this below stairs. Do you understand?" *Perhaps we may keep the lady's reputation intact if we can limit the gossip.*

Sarah's eyes were wide. "Yes, sir."

"Excellent. I shall arrange for another maid to sit with you and the physician in case he needs to send one of you for something during the night. I am returning to my chambers. Roberts will keep me apprised of Miss Elizabeth's health."

"Shall I assist you back to your rooms, sir?" asked the valet.

"I think I can manage. Beckett, shall we go?" *I will not show weakness in front of this man.*

Beckett's blue eyes were cold. "Lead the way."

Darcy's ire gave him strength as he walked the short distance to his chambers. He led Beckett to his sitting room rather than his bedchamber and stood behind a chair, using his hands to steady himself.

As soon as Beckett closed the door, Darcy took control of the conversation.

"Why were you at Oakham Mount with Miss Elizabeth?"

Beckett glared at him. "If you must know, I was following her."

"So you admit it! What were you about, man? She is a gentleman's daughter. Do you wish to ruin her? Were you having an assignation with her?" Darcy kept his voice to a low growl with great effort. He did not wish for anyone else to hear the conversation.

The physician's blue eyes flashed. "I was up before sunrise this morning to see to my patients, and I found Miss Bennet asleep in her chambers with only a maid who slumbered, as well. When I woke the girl and asked her where Miss Elizabeth was, she told me the young lady had left before sunrise to walk. The maid alerted me when Miss Elizabeth again left the house by herself an hour or so ago, so I quickly left the house and saw her entering the woods alone. It was dark, and I feared for her safety, so I followed her. There was no assignation. She had no idea I was behind her, and I fully intended to keep my presence a secret."

Darcy breathed deeply, hoping to calm his temper. "How did she acquire an injury?"

Beckett ran his hands through his hair. "She must have heard me behind her, for she began to flee through the woods. I thought she might fall, so I ran after her, calling her name to let her know she was in no danger. Just as I was about to reach her, she tripped over something, hitting her head on a rock. I could not leave her there in such a condition while I came back for help. I removed her bonnet and found evidence of a head injury. When she awoke from her faint, she did not know me."

"And you thought carrying her to a house full of people was the best way to protect her character? How did you arrive at that brilliant conclusion?"

Beckett's jaw hardened. "I was concerned for her health more than her reputation. She was confused and crying. She could not walk. It was my fault she ran and fell, and I tried to make it right."

Darcy tilted his head, thinking through everything the physician said. "She cried because she was in terrible pain?"

"She cried because of you, ingrate!" Beckett spat in anger. "She did not remember me, but she remembered you and your hateful words. I suspect what you said will ring in her mind for many years. I highly doubt she would have been out in the dark had you not insulted her. I should call you out."

"You forget yourself, but I shall overlook it this once," Darcy said, eyes blazing at him. "What hateful words? I have spoken very little with Miss Elizabeth, and I remember every word we have ever exchanged. She must have been talking out of her head. After all, she called you an angel."

"I forget myself? I think not." Beckett's voice rose. "When I picked her up from the ground, she said I must put her down, for she was too heavy for me to carry. She said you refused to dance with her on those grounds. Was she wrong? I would dearly love to think you would not hurt any young woman in that way. However, having observed her briskly walking on two occasions when she should have been safely in the house because of the darkness, I tend to think she is attempting to exercise as a means of becoming smaller in size. When I first met her, I noticed her dress was rather loose, as if she had been losing weight. After I came to that conclusion, I watched what she ate at dinner. It was almost nothing. I further concluded that she said nothing undeserved of you. You have always been a proud man. You think too highly of yourself and too meanly of others."

The gentleman's face blanched. *Dear Lord. It is my fault that she is injured. What else has she suffered through my thoughtlessness?* He looked away. "I did say that, but I have heartily regretted it. I hoped that she did not take it to heart, for I admire her a great deal."

"You admire her?" Beckett's chiseled features were set in stone. "Do not worry about Miss Elizabeth's reputation, for I assure you, I could love the lady quite easily. If she is considered to be compromised, I will gladly offer for her, praying she will accept me. Marrying a beautiful, kind-hearted, intelligent woman has long been my dream. Not only is she physically lovely, but she houses an equally lovely soul. I have looked for a lady like her for several years, but no one has caught my eye until now."

Darcy's heart sank. "Would your family accept her? She has almost no dowry, and her connections to trade would likely displease your father or brother."

Beckett laughed. "My father is a duke and my brother a marquess. I am but an earl, a title given to me by King George to reward my father for his assistance in the war. I do not need to marry for status or wealth, for I have both already, and they are cold company. My family would approve her lively disposition and faithfulness to those she loves. To be among that select group would be my honour."

Darcy moved to the front of the chair and sat down, weary to the bone. "How did I not know you are an earl? We have been friends for many years."

"I have never felt the need to share the information. I enjoy being a physician. Declaring my connections and monetary worth would interfere with my profession. Who would call an earl to heal them? In addition, I would become a target for mercenary mamas and their society daughters. That prospect is unattractive to me. I would much rather marry a gentlewoman such as Miss Elizabeth or Miss Bennet."

He has not decided on Miss Elizabeth if he names her sister in the same breath.

Darcy's outlook brightened considerably.

ROBIN HELM

CHAPTER 11

He has no form or comeliness; and when we see Him, there is no beauty that we should desire Him.
Isaiah 53:2b

Elizabeth opened her eyes slowly, wondering where she was. She lifted her head and glanced around the room. Her gaze came to rest on Mr. Beckett, asleep on a chaise not three feet from the side of her bed.

She could not look away from his unblemished beauty. The man was incomparable in both his face and his form. *He is striking beyond anyone else I have ever seen.*

Her mind soon took a different path. *Why is he here with me instead of with Jane or Mr. Darcy?*

Sarah sat in a chair next to him, watching her. She stood and came to Elizabeth's side. "Oh, you are finally awake!"

The maid turned to tap the physician's shoulder before Elizabeth could stop her. He immediately opened his eyes, catching her staring at him before she could focus on anything else.

She blushed furiously.

The young man stood, smiling, and walked the short distance to her. He put his hand on her forehead, carefully moving it through her hair to the side of her head, using his fingers to touch her gently.

Elizabeth winced, and he withdrew his hand, resting it on her pillow.

"How do you feel this morning?" he asked softly.

"My head is sore where you touched it," she admitted. "Why are you here? Is Jane well?"

His blue eyes twinkled. "You are my principal patient now, for your sister and Darcy are much better. One more day of rest should restore them to full health."

She attempted to sit up, but Mr. Beckett shook his head. "You should not try that just yet. You took a hard bump to your head, and I feel certain it still pains you. Miss Bennet is being cared for very well, for your mother came from Longbourn to tend her."

"Mama is here? Why?"

"Mr. Bingley rode to Longbourn the night you were injured, and she and your father came at daybreak the following morning. Mr. Bennet returned home yesterday afternoon to be with your younger sisters once he saw both you and Miss Bennet were healing properly."

Elizabeth's expression betrayed her shock. "My last memory is of running through the woods towards Oakham Mount. How long ago was that?"

He took a deep breath. "That was two nights ago. I kept you awake for the remainder of the first night, but you slept most of yesterday and last night. This is the first time you recognized me."

"What happened?" she asked.

"Are you hungry?" He looked behind him at Sarah, then returned his attention to Elizabeth. "You have eaten hardly anything for two nights and a day."

He wants to talk to me alone? "Yes, I think I could eat some eggs and toast."

"Sarah," he said, glancing back at her. "Please go down to the kitchen. Tell Mrs. Brooks to give you a tray for Miss Elizabeth. Be sure to have a pot of tea and two cups."

Sarah hurried out and closed the door behind her.

Elizabeth cleared her throat. "Should we be together unattended, sir?"

"Susan sleeps on the couch." He pointed to the other side of the bed, whispering. "See? Propriety is being satisfied."

"Why have you sent Sarah away?"

He looked down at his hands, and his long eyelashes fanned against his cheeks. "Partly because you really should eat, and partly because I do not wish for an audience when I relay how you were injured."

"Should I be concerned?" *Please tell me I did not humiliate myself.*

"No, not at all, though you may be unhappy with me." He did not raise his eyes.

Whatever could be wrong? "I have found the best course is usually the straightforward one. Simply tell me what happened. I feel sure you were not at fault, whatever happened."

He took a deep breath, and the words began to tumble out. "I went to your sister's room before sunrise two days ago, but you were not there. The maid told me you had gone out walking." A flush crept up his neck. "I had already noticed your dresses were a bit loose." His blush deepened further. "Please forgive me. I am a physician, and it is my habit to assess the health of the people I meet. I know it sounds impertinent. I am embarrassed myself when I say the words, but I did notice your appearance."

She smiled wanly. "That is not unusual, especially in my case, so do not berate yourself, Mr. Beckett. I am quite accustomed to it." *He, too, finds me wanting.*

He groaned aloud. "No, I think you misunderstand entirely. Allow me to explain. You are a very beautiful woman and a gentleman's daughter. 'Tis unusual for a lady in your position to wear clothes that do not fit properly. I had my suspicions, so I watched you at dinner. When you ate very little, I thought you must be trying to attain a smaller size, though I could not understand why. You are perfectly lovely as you are."

She bit her lower lip. *He cannot mean that. What is he hiding?* "Pray, continue."

Mr. Beckett shifted uneasily from one foot to the other. "Late that night I went to your sister's room looking for you. When you were absent again, I asked the maid where you were, and she said you had gone walking alone, so I hurried to follow you. I was worried that you might come to harm out in the woods by yourself at night. There was a full moon, but it was dark in the trees. I thought I could hide my presence from you, but I must have made a noise, for you began to run. I raced after you, calling out so you would stop, but you only ran faster. I must have frightened you most dreadfully, though I never meant to do so."

He ran both hands through his thick, wavy hair, obviously agitated.

She reached a hand towards him. "Do not be distressed. You meant well. I truly believe you had no idea of alarming me. In truth, I barely remember it. Did I fall?"

His eyes were tortured as he looked at her. "I had nearly caught up with you when I saw you sail headlong into a large rock. You were not moving. I thought you were dead." His breath caught. "You cannot imagine how terrible I felt, thinking that the terror you ran from was me – that I was responsible for your death."

"Give me your hand," she entreated, reaching towards him. When he took her hand in his, she continued. "You did nothing wrong. You were seeking my safety. I thank you. No one outside my own family has ever showed such concern for me before now."

"I have not finished. You may not be so generous when I tell you all."

"Then, finish. What happened that night is in the past. I will deal with the consequences of my own rash actions. I should not have been walking alone in the woods at night."

He held her hand more tightly. "I took off your bonnet and pulled the pins from your hair so I could ascertain if you were injured. When I found the lump on the side of your head, I realized you likely had suffered a concussion. You awoke and confirmed my suspicions, for you were speaking freely in a way you never would have, were you still in your right mind." He paused.

Elizabeth squeezed his hand. "What did I say?"

He looked away. "You called me an angel, and when I took you in my arms to carry you, you began to cry and told me what Darcy had said about you."

Mr. Becket turned back to her, his eyes piercing her. "I was so angry at him, I did not think how it might appear to anyone who saw me enter Netherfield with you cradled against my chest. To be completely truthful, I did not care. I did not even realize it until Darcy himself confronted me."

Her eyes were round. "Mr. Darcy! What did he say?"

Mr. Beckett released her and hung his head, covering his face with his hands. "He rightly said I may have placed you in an untenable position. Please forgive me."

Tears rolled down her cheeks, and she hastily wiped them away. *He fears he has compromised me, and he does not wish to marry me. I refuse to trap a good man into marriage, no matter how attractive he is to me.*

"Do not be anxious, Mr. Beckett." She choked on the words. "If there is talk, I do not expect you to do anything. You owe me nothing for helping me. Gossip will die down soon enough."

"No, no! You misunderstand me," he said, looking up at her in alarm. "I do not fear for myself. I care only that you may be forced into something you do not wish to do. I would be happy to – "

A footman opened the door, and Sarah entered the room, carrying a tray. She placed it on the table and curtseyed. "You are wanted in the library, sir. Mr. Bingley wishes to speak with you at once."

"Tell him I will be with him shortly," answered the physician.

Sarah shook her head. "Mr. Bingley said it was urgent. 'Tis a matter which cannot be delayed for even a moment. A matter of life or death. He told me to tell you that."

Mr. Beckett sighed, rubbing his forehead. "I must go talk to him, but I shall return as soon as I can. Wait for me, I beg of you.

This conversation is not finished. Surely I shan't be gone more than an hour or two."

"On a matter of life or death?" she answered, smiling.

"With Bingley, everything is always a matter of life or death. Please, I promise you I shall be back very soon."

She gestured to the bed. "It appears I have no plans for the day; I am a captive audience. Go solve the problems of the world. I shall wait here for you."

He took her hand, bent over it, and kissed her knuckles softly before he left the room.

Elizabeth thought back over their conversation, musing over each exchange, until she decided there was no way to know what he wished to say.

Guessing will only serve to bring me pain should I be wrong. He said he would return quickly, and he is a man of his word.

She waited patiently as the long hours of the morning passed, unable to concentrate enough to read, but unwilling to ask a servant for the whereabouts of Mr. Beckett. She napped through the afternoon, but as the darkness began to fall, Mrs. Bennet entered her chambers, preceding Sarah who carried Elizabeth's dinner.

"My dear, you are awake!" she exclaimed crossing the room to embrace her daughter. "Are you hungry?"

Elizabeth found comfort in her mother's arms. "I think I can eat a bit. How is Jane?"

Mrs. Bennet kissed her cheek and released her. "She is quite well, my dear, and as the physician has agreed, we shall all go back to Longbourn in the morning."

Sarah placed the tray on the table, and Mrs. Bennet began to feed Elizabeth, talking with great animation.

"The militia has come to be stationed in Meryton, and Mr. Bennet's cousin, Mr. Collins is coming to call. We must make a good impression, for he will inherit Longbourn once your father passes."

"Mr. Beckett gave permission for me to return home?" asked Elizabeth.

"Oh, yes, my love! I saw him this morning before he left to return to London. In such a hurry, but young men always are. Such a fine gentleman. Very handsome, indeed."

Elizabeth turned her face to the wall, refusing to eat anything else.

After a few minutes of trying unsuccessfully to get her daughter to take more nourishment, her mother left, saying she was to join the Bingleys for dinner.

Elizabeth welcomed the silence as her tears came.

He promised he would return, but he did not.

ROBIN HELM

CHAPTER 12

I will praise You, for I am fearfully and wonderfully made.
Psalm 139:4

Mid-morning the following day, Darcy and Bingley waited in the great hall of Netherfield to bid farewell to the Bennet sisters and their mother.

Mrs. Bennet preceded Jane and Elizabeth down the stairway, smiling at the gentlemen. "Both of you must dine with us this evening. I shall not take 'no' for an answer, so do not attempt to refuse me. I must thank you properly for taking such superb care of my daughters. Mr. Bingley, your sisters and Mr. Hurst would be welcomed, as well."

While Mr. Bingley accepted for himself and Darcy, the latter gentleman watched Elizabeth with growing concern.

She looks drawn and pale, and she has grown so thin her pelisse and dress hang loosely from her frame. There are dark circles under her eyes.

He frowned. *Has she completely stopped sleeping and eating?* The man nearly growled in frustration. *This is my doing. My stupidity in making that remark is the cause of all this. She was perfectly happy until I entered her sphere.*

As she reached the bottom of the stairs, he stepped forward and offered her his arm for support.

Mrs. Bennet was holding court at the front door, and Darcy felt certain he could speak quietly for a few moments with the young lady without being too closely observed.

"Miss Elizabeth, are you sure you feel well enough to travel? I would not have you further risk your health by hurrying away from Netherfield before you are completely healed."

She lifted her eyes to his as she took his arm. "I thank you for your concern, sir, but I am quite eager to return home. I shall rest better in my own bed."

Her eyes were filled with pain; her voice held none of its usual liveliness.

Darcy knew he had hurt her, and he longed to make it right.

He attempted a smile. "Your mother has invited Bingley and me to dine at Longbourn tonight. I miss our spirited conversations, for no one but you speaks so frankly to me. Will you promise to attend?"

She shook her head. "I no longer believe in promises, but I will be there. Mama would not allow it to be otherwise."

She no longer believes in promises? Is this Beckett's doing?

"Miss Elizabeth, if I should arrive an hour before dinner at Longbourn, would you sit in the gardens with me?"

"I require a chaperone, Mr. Darcy," she replied firmly. "You know my situation only too well. From now on, I will strictly obey every rule of convention, for I refuse to give my family further cause for concern or humiliation."

"Of course," he answered with a nod. "Would Mr. Bingley and your sister satisfy your requirements? I could make certain we are always in view of each other. I have no intention of exposing you or your sister to censure."

She tilted her head and looked at him as if she could see into his soul. "No, I never thought you would, Mr. Darcy, but lately I have realized I am a poor judge of character. I no longer trust myself where people, especially men, are concerned. You may be a rogue, and I would never see it."

He thought she might be joking, so he waited to see if she would smile, but she did not. "I think you judge yourself far too harshly. Will you agree to talk with me before we dine?"

"If Jane and Mr. Bingley are in agreement, I shall walk in the gardens with you at Longbourn. We also have a little wilderness you might enjoy. I go there when I am in need of solitude, but I believe we might agree on the beauty of the place."

His broad smile was genuine. "I do find a measure of peace in untamed nature. I shall look forward to exploring it with you."

Mrs. Bennet's voice rang out. "Come, Elizabeth. The carriage awaits."

Mr. Darcy accompanied her to the carriage and gave her his hand to make certain she entered safely. He stepped back, his full attention on Elizabeth as the conveyance pulled away, watching until it was out of sight.

Mr. Bingley stepped up beside him. "Do you fancy a ride into Meryton? We never did go to the bookseller's shop, and Miss Elizabeth's books travel back to Longbourn with her." He looked up. "The sky is clear. I think we may safely go on horseback. Xanthos likely needs to run, for no one apart from you dares to ride him. I heard from my man that the stable boys all live in terror of the monster."

Darcy nodded, chuckling. "A fine idea. Let me get my boots and coat. Since the stable boys are afraid, I shall saddle Xanthos myself. The beast has been penned up too long. After a hard ride, he will be less likely to bite your servants."

Within half an hour, the two gentlemen, along with Mr. Hurst, were on the road to Meryton, Darcy's golden stallion leading the way.

Darcy was hidden from view in the bookshelves of the book store when he heard two ladies talking.

"Lady Lucas, did you hear the news? I was told just this morning that there will be a wedding at Longbourn."

He furrowed his brow. *A wedding at Longbourn? One of Miss Elizabeth's sisters? Surely someone would have mentioned it.*

"No, Mrs. Long. You must be mistaken, for my Charlotte would have told me were any of the Bennets entertaining the idea of marriage. She and Maria are great friends with the Bennet girls, you know."

"It must be so. One of the Netherfield footmen is seeing my cook's daughter. He told her the young physician who came from London carried the second Bennet girl, Elizabeth, into the house a few nights ago. They had been alone at Oakham Mount when she fell and was injured, and the young man held her, sleeping in his arms, as if she were a child, clutched to his chest. Elizabeth has always been the most sensible of the sisters. She would never allow such intimacy with a man who was not her fiancé."

"But, Mrs. Long, if Elizabeth was not awake, perhaps she hit her head. She might not have known he was carrying her."

He closed his eyes. *Perhaps it will be well. Lady Lucas may be able to stop the rumours.*

"You may be right, Lady Lucas, but I heard he was in her room unchaperoned. He sent the maid away on an errand, and they were alone. Surely they are betrothed."

"My Charlotte will visit her tomorrow, then, and we shall know the truth of it. Good day, Mrs. Long."

"Good day to you, Lady Lucas."

Darcy's heart sank. *Miss Elizabeth will be ruined, and Beckett is gone. How will she bear it? She said she no longer believed in promises. Did he promise her something before he left?*

His sympathy for the lady was soon overridden by his fury and indignation directed at the physician. *How could he leave her in such a circumstance with no explanation to any of us?*

Darcy thought back through Elizabeth's words. *He must have promised marriage, but then decided against marrying her and fled. Could he be a rogue? None of us saw that in him, if he is.*

He tried to envision a way to force Beckett to marry her, but every thought made him more miserable.

I would not have her marry a man who does not wish to wed her. She deserves to be happy.

However, he knew she would have to wed, and very soon, or her sisters would be ostracized, as well. Her entire family would be disgraced, shunned by polite society.

There is nothing else for it. I brought him to Netherfield, and it was due to my hurtful remark she was walking that night. I must marry her.

Once the idea had taken root in his mind, Darcy began to think of the advantages – and there were many. The disadvantages were few in comparison, small in consequence, and mostly eliminated by moving her to Pemberley.

The rather austere gentleman found that he quite liked the idea of wedding lovely, vivacious Elizabeth Bennet, and he spent a full hour imagining the joy he would bring her by asking for her hand.

As Bingley's sisters and brother-in-law had declined the invitation to Longbourn, Darcy and Bingley arrived an hour early for dinner with no difficulty.

They were received with great civility by Mrs. Bennet, and she acquiesced most graciously when Bingley requested that Miss Bennet and Miss Elizabeth show them the gardens.

Darcy, true to his word, had arranged beforehand with Bingley that they would always be within sight of one another. Bingley had been happy to agree.

The four of them made a congenial party as they walked towards the flowers and shrubs.

When Darcy asked Elizabeth to sit with him among the rose arbors, Bingley did the same with Jane, though he was careful to guide her far enough way to prevent either couple from being overheard.

"Are you feeling better today?" Darcy asked, leaning forward to view her expression.

"I am much improved, thank you. Have you fully recovered?"

He smiled. "Indeed, I am. I felt well enough to ride this morning, and I put Xanthos through his paces with a punishing ride to Meryton."

She turned her face towards him, and he relaxed into the back of the bench.

"Xanthos?" she asked with a small smile. "Named for Achilles's immortal horse that had the ability to speak?"

Darcy chuckled, encouraged by her expression. "My stallion. His ill temper meant no one would ride him while I was unable to do so."

"Do you normally ride daily?"

He nodded. "Yes, I enjoy the exercise every morning and evening."

"Interesting. My sister and I walk at sunrise and again at sunset."

"I may have seen you at Oakham Mount on one or two occasions."

Her gaze sharpened. "I have observed a man on a large horse several times. I must learn to be more careful. Had you been a man of dubious intentions, my sister and I might have been in some danger."

Darcy nodded. "While I dislike that idea, I must agree." He took a deep breath. "In fact, I fear you have already encountered some trouble."

She looked at her hands, clasped in her lap. "Whatever could you mean?"

"You were injured in more ways than one by your fall at Oakham Mount."

Elizabeth lowered her eyes. "What do you mean, sir?"

"I overheard a conversation between two ladies at the bookstore this morning."

She turned her face towards his. "I assume it must have had something to do with me and Mr. Beckett."

"Yes," he replied solemnly. "Mrs. Long was telling Lady Lucas about your accident, including how the physician carried you back to Netherfield. She also knew you had been alone with him in your room."

Elizabeth looked away.

Unable to see her face, Darcy continued. "Lady Lucas defended you, but she shall send her daughter here tomorrow to determine if the story is true."

"To my knowledge, I was not alone with him in my chambers, and I have no memory of Mr. Beckett carrying me to Netherfield. I never had the power of refusal in either instance."

Darcy shook his head. "Indeed, you were unaware of it, but I saw for myself that you were unchaperoned with him. I talked to Beckett, pointing out the impropriety – the damage he might have done to your reputation by sending Sarah away. In the other instance, the entire house witnessed his return from Oakham Mount with you in his arms."

She rubbed her forehead and glanced at him. "I have done nothing wrong, yet I am condemned for it. If you lay blame at my feet, and you were there, how will I ever prove my innocence?"

"I do not blame you!" he replied, lightly touching her arm. "Others were at fault, but not you. Are you determined to continue walking morning and night, starving yourself because of what I said at the Assembly?"

"How much humiliation must I bear?" Elizabeth cried, rising quickly. "Yes. Are you satisfied?"

"Please," he answered, standing beside her. "Stay a moment. I must finish what I have to say."

She crossed her arms and looked away.

"This is all properly laid at my door," he said. "You would never have gone walking alone at night had I not made those ridiculous, unfounded remarks."

He heard her sound of disgust and decided to change his approach.

"Did Beckett promise you anything before he left?" *Are they engaged?*

Elizabeth nodded. "Mr. Beckett was talking to me when he was called downstairs, and he promised he would return to me as soon as he could. He said it would be no more than an hour or two."

"And he did not?"

She shook her head. "I waited all day with no word from him. Last night, my mother told me he had returned to London."

"Did he not leave you a note?"

Her voice was so quiet, he could hardly hear it. "No, I had nothing from him."

Darcy would have preferred to keep his information to himself, but that would have been deceitful, and he abhorred deceit.

"Beckett received an express and left nearly immediately, telling none of us why. I know it must have been something terrible for him to behave in such a fashion. However, he took a moment to scribble a note. I saw it myself on the salver. It was sealed – directed to you. Did you not receive it?"

Elizabeth turned to face him. "I did not, but 'tis no matter. He could have come himself in the time it took to write to me. This changes nothing. He is gone, and I must bear the consequences of his actions."

Darcy sighed. "May I ask what you will do?"

She lifted her chin. "I shall leave tomorrow to stay with my aunt and uncle in Cheapside. Perhaps if I am gone, the gossip will die down."

"The fault is mine, and so must the remedy be. I shall make it right."

Elizabeth stared at him, eyebrows raised. "And how do you plan to do that, sir?"

He cleared his throat and swallowed.

"I will marry you."

CHAPTER 13

He who answers a matter before he hears it, it is folly and shame to
him.
Proverbs 18:13

Elizabeth's mouth dropped open in astonishment. *Did he say he*
will marry me?

"Well?" he asked.

"I must beg your pardon, sir. Was that a question or a
statement?" she returned. "I confess I am confused."

Darcy knit his brows. "I said, 'I will marry you.' What confuses
you?"

"Perhaps I wondered whether you require an answer or not, as I
did not hear you ask a question."

Shaking his head, the gentleman looked heavenward. "Of
course. I have never before asked any woman to consent to be my
wife. Forgive my awkwardness, as I have no experience in the art."

She looked at him, bemused. "Why are you offering to marry
me? Is it due to a sense of guilt or obligation? Are you the patron
saint of stained reputations?"

He stood tall, clasping his hands behind his back. "I caused this
entire situation by making that absurd remark at the Assembly. Had I
kept my thoughts to myself, you would not have been determined to
walk at night."

"True, perhaps, but I would still be 'too much to tempt you' had you not said it. Would you have agreed to marry me had I not begun walking and started moderating the amounts that I ate?"

"I can answer only to the present circumstances," he replied. "I did not know you – I had never even met you – when I made that insulting comment, but now that I have spent some time with you, I think differently."

"Differently enough that you would have asked the same question of me were I not in this predicament?" she asked, looking straight into his eyes.

He refuses to be entirely candid.

"Why does it matter?" He raised his brows. "I am asking you now. That is the material point."

She stood, sighing. "Because it matters to me. I do not wish to wed a man who loves me only when I am thin, for I may increase again when I am happily married with children or as I age."

He shook his head. "I assure you, I can admire you in all your forms. 'Tis more likely we shall grow old and fat together than to think I would base my affections on your waistline."

"I do not want to feel my husband did me a favour in marrying me, whether it was for my situation, my reputation, or my figure. My looks will fade. Will you love me then?"

His voice was low. "I am fully aware I am not an easy man to know. I have not the pleasant manners of my friend Bingley, nor the striking good looks and easy charm of Beckett. Not many people understand me, and fewer still truly like me for myself. If you can care for me as I am, you shall certainly have my adoration."

Elizabeth paused before continuing. "Very well. You have stated you will marry me. You never asked me if I want to marry you. I told you once before, only the strongest love will induce me into matrimony. You would wed me to spare me the disgrace of being compromised. You speak of admiration, adoration, care, but not love. While I appreciate your willingness to protect me and my family, I have no desire to live my life as the wife of a man who values me as a friend but does not love me. I imagine you would prefer a wife who loves you, as well. You said as much when I was reading to you."

Darcy dropped his hands to his sides, looking at the ground. "Am I so unlovable? Could you not learn to love me?"

"Mr. Darcy," she said softly.

He looked up, his eyes hopeful.

She continued. "I never said you were unlovable. Perhaps my feelings for you would grow if we knew each other better. I already think of you as honourable and good, and I believe we have much in common. I suppose my question is, could you love a woman whose reputation is not pristine? I know you are proud, and people will gossip. You must have some reservations about the match."

Darcy lifted his chin. "I do not worry concerning what people will say, but I truly have no wish to marry a woman who loves another man. That is my only reservation. Are you in love with Thaddeus Beckett? I hold you in highest esteem, and I know you will be truthful with me. As long as you do not love him, I think I could find no other woman who pleases me so much as you do."

She smiled. "Perhaps I could have grown to love him, but I do not."

He exhaled. "Marry me," he pleaded.

"Why?"

"Why? Because we read the same books, and you disagree with me more often than not. Because you are lovely and kind. Because my money does not impress you. Because you fascinate me. Is that not enough? Marry me."

Elizabeth chuckled. "I cannot agree to marry you today. Shall we test the strength of our feelings by waiting to become betrothed? By tomorrow, I shall likely bear the mark of a ruined woman. If you still wish to marry me in a month, ask me again."

"What if Beckett comes back?"

Is that fear in his eyes? she wondered.

"I doubt he will, but what if he does? I have told you I do not love him. If we agree to a month's courtship, I promise you I will consider no other men while you and I get to know each other better."

Darcy's brilliant smile nearly blinded her.

"Then you agree to a courtship?" he asked eagerly. "And you will accept me at the end of it?"

She nodded. "In a month, if you can truthfully say you love me, I will accept your offer."

He looked at her thoughtfully. "But what if you still do not love me?"

She looked at him from the corner of her eye. "I am but a simple country maiden, Mr. Darcy. Do you think I could resist a worthy, handsome, intelligent man who loves me and does his best to win my love?"

"Probably not, and if such a man appears in Meryton in the next month, I hope you do not meet him."

Elizabeth laughed aloud.

"Ah! I have made you laugh, and I heard you say you dearly love to laugh." Darcy smiled at her. "If I make you laugh every day for a month, I think you will love me."

She was suddenly sober. "As long as you do not make me cry, as well."

He started to reach for her hand but seemed to think better of it. "I made you cry once, but I did not like it. I shall endeavour never to do so again."

"'Tis nearly time for us to go in to dinner."

"Stay a moment. We have an unusual arrangement, and I wish to make an unusual request."

Curious. "State your request."

He bit his lower lip. "I wish to speak to your father and let him know my intentions are entirely honourable. I would like his approval of the conditions of the courtship."

Nodding, she replied, "That is reasonable. Why would you think I would not agree?"

"Because I should like for you to confide to Miss Lucas, when she calls tomorrow, that we are in a courtship. Normally, you would not share such information until we are engaged."

"You wish to protect my reputation?"

"Not necessarily; at least, that is not my principal concern. I confess I want others to know you and I have an understanding of sorts. Miss Lucas need not share her knowledge with others, if you wish to keep it secret, though she could say she knows for a fact you are not unmarriageable and have had an offer from a suitable gentleman, which you are considering."

He is ashamed of me. "You do not wish to marry a woman connected with scandal."

"How can you think that?" he asked, shaking his head. "In the past half hour, I have asked you three times to marry me. This is not so much to protect you as it is to stake my claim. I am a selfish, jealous man where you are concerned. For one month at least, you are mine. Other men would know not to interfere."

Mr. Darcy is rather sweet. Who would have thought it? "Then talk to my father. If he agrees, I shall confide in Charlotte tomorrow."

Darcy's smile was triumphant as he offered her his arm, and she slipped her hand into the crook of his elbow.

After a lovely meal, Darcy requested an audience with Mr. Bennet. As the gentlemen walked towards the library, Darcy looked back, secured Elizabeth's attention, and gestured for her to come with them.

Once they were all in the room, Elizabeth closed the door and joined Darcy before her father's desk.

When they were seated, Mr. Bennet leaned forward, looking at Darcy with interest. "You wished to speak with me?"

Darcy took a deep breath. "Yes. I have asked Miss Elizabeth to marry me, and she has given me her answer."

The elder gentleman leaned forward, placing his elbows on the desk and steepling his fingers. "And what am I to do? If she has given you her consent, I shall not oppose her wishes."

The young man grimaced. "Her consent. About that. We find ourselves in a situation which is different from most betrothals." He glanced at Elizabeth. "She has placed a stipulation upon her acceptance of my offer."

Mr. Bennet directed his attention to his daughter with open curiosity. "Stipulation? Explain, please, Lizzy."

"I have asked for a month's courtship before I agree to the betrothal. I should like to know Mr. Darcy better before I accept. Therefore, I would prefer we kept this among us three."

He turned back to Darcy. "I dislike secrecy, and I should think you would prefer transparency, as well. Why would you allow such a thing? Are you embarrassed to be engaged to my daughter?"

"Not at all. I would gladly marry her tomorrow, though I understand her reasons."

"In truth?" asked Mr. Bennet, peering over his glasses at the young man. "Enlighten me."

Darcy looked at his hands. "I made an insulting remark about Miss Elizabeth before I ever met her. She overheard it. I am quite ashamed of myself."

"All of us know you slighted my Lizzy. There must be more to this than that."

"That unfortunate incident precipitated a series of events which will lead to public censure of your daughter by tomorrow," Darcy replied, raising his eyes to Mr. Bennet's face. "There is already gossip. I heard two ladies talking in the Meryton bookshop. As I am the one at fault, I should provide the solution to the problem."

"Lizzy?"

She blushed. "I am considered to be compromised, though I did nothing wrong."

Mr. Bennet stood, voice rising, fists clenched. "You have ruined my daughter?"

Darcy held up his hands. "I did not. Beckett, my physician, followed her from Netherfield to Oakham Mount a few nights ago, hoping to protect her without her knowledge. She heard a noise behind her and, frightened, ran through the trees in the dark. In the process, she fell and injured her head. Since she could not walk and, in fact, was not able to reason enough to help herself, Beckett carried her back to Netherfield. He was also alone with her in her chambers there when he sent the maid on an errand. Your daughter does not remember either of those occurrences."

"And why is this your fault, Mr. Darcy? It seems to me that Mr. Beckett should be sitting where you are." He sat down, glaring across his desk.

"She would not have been walking alone at night had I kept my opinions to myself. Beckett is gone, but I would offer for your daughter in any case. I have a very high regard for her."

"Hmmm…." Mr. Bennet looked between them. "How would your courtship protect her when she insists on secrecy?"

"Lady Lucas will send her daughter here tomorrow to learn what she can of the matter. I asked Miss Elizabeth to convince her that she is considering an eligible match from a gentleman of means. When we announce our betrothal in a month, everyone will know I am the suitor."

"So, you are the obstacle to an immediate public betrothal, Lizzy?" he asked. "You know you shall have to marry. Why not go forward with the plan now?"

"I had always hoped to marry for love," she replied, tears in her eyes.

Her father's eyes were sad. "You could have a yearlong courtship, but it would not guarantee love that is lasting."

"Please, Father." Her eyes beseeched him. "Allow me to do this my way."

Mr. Bennet nodded slowly. "Very well. I will agree on one condition."

"Name it," said Darcy.

"If any scandal attaches to Lizzy's name, you will marry at once."

Darcy smiled. "At once. I agree."

Elizabeth swallowed. "Thank you, Father. I will do as you ask."

I may be married within a week if I cannot convince Charlotte to help me.

She glanced at Darcy, admiring his dark good looks.

Marriage to such a man could be very pleasant. I can imagine much worse things.

CHAPTER 14

*And as ye would that men should do to you, do ye also to them
likewise.*
Luke 6:31

Darcy was up before sunrise the following morning, hoping to
catch a glimpse of Elizabeth as she took her customary walk to
Oakham Mount. Before half an hour had passed, he was dressed,
mounted on Xanthos, and galloping towards his goal.

Seeing Elizabeth and her sister climbing the hill, he dismounted
and tied the horse's reins to a tree. Soon, the gentleman was striding
towards the ladies.

Upon reaching them, he bowed quickly, then turned to walk
with them, placing himself between the sisters.

"Good morning, Miss Bennet, Miss Elizabeth."

Jane was serene. "Good morning, sir."

Elizabeth was busily trying to stuff her curls under her bonnet.
"I am not fit to be seen," she muttered.

"Leave it," he said softly. "I have seen your hair down on
several occasions. 'Tis quite beautiful."

She glanced up at him, colouring. "'Tis quite improper, you
mean."

"After the first time I saw your lovely hair unbound, catching
the sun as you ran down the hill, I tried to be here morning and night,

hoping for the same view again. How could something so magnificent be improper?"

Jane's quiet laugh caught his attention, and he was unsurprised to see her smiling. She increased her pace to walk a little distance ahead of them.

He dipped his head, whispering to Elizabeth, "Have you told your sister?"

She nodded, flashing her green eyes at him. "I practiced on her."

Darcy chuckled. "Practiced?"

"I must speak with Charlotte this morning, and I wanted to fix in my mind what I should say." She blew out her breath. "Our situation is most unconventional, so I wished to prepare myself for her inevitable questions. Jane played the part of Charlotte. She was a great help, for she knows us both very well."

"Will you tell her all? I would have her know I am your suitor."

"Good, for I see no other way to waylay the rumours. To Charlotte, at least, my intended must be flesh-and-blood. She can be more convincing in defence of my honour if she knows the facts in the case."

Darcy lowered his voice. "I should like to pay you a visit this afternoon or evening to learn the results of your conversation with your friend. We would be chaperoned, as Bingley is most willing to accompany me and talk with your sister."

Elizabeth glanced up at him, her eyes narrowed. "Would you use your friend to entice me into agreeing with your plan?"

"Not at all," he replied calmly. "My friend enjoys the company of your sister. I rather think he is using me more than I am using him. He has offered his services more than once."

"And you have no objection to a match between them?"

He raised a brow. "That would be rather hypocritical, would it not? If I have offered for you, I obviously do not object to connecting your family to mine. How could I then justify disapproval of a marriage between Bingley and Miss Bennet?"

"I cannot think you held that opinion even last week," she said, shaking her head. "In fact, I overheard a servant saying you warned

Mr. Bingley that a union with my sister would damage his sister's marriage prospects."

Darcy cleared his throat. "I will always endeavour to be honest with you. I believe my first words in that conversation were that your sister is lovely, kind, and all that a gentleman's daughter should be. When pressed, I did say it was possible a marriage between the two of them might damage Caroline's chances of making a good match. However, after I observed how much Bingley truly admired Miss Bennet, I told him Caroline's fortune could secure her a match with one of the large number of impoverished noblemen we know. I also told him I would have nothing further to say on the matter, and I have kept my word. Do you believe me?"

As they were in view of Longbourn, Elizabeth stopped and turned to him. "I do," she replied, gazing at him. "You are the most honourable man of my acquaintance."

She trusts me. He was much encouraged. "May I come to you later today?"

"I think Charlotte will visit during the morning hours, but I cannot be certain. We are close friends and do not always follow the rules of society with one another. She may come this afternoon instead, if she has something else she must do first."

The gentleman remained silent, bowing his head, trying to hide his disappointment.

After a moment, he heard her sweet voice. "You know Jane and I walk in the evenings as well as the mornings. Meet us at Oakham Mount just before the sun sets, and I shall tell you what you wish to know."

"So, you have changed your usual time to walk?" he asked, lifting his face to hers. "I was hoping you no longer walked in the darkness. 'Tis dangerous, especially if anyone unscrupulous should notice your habits, as I have."

"You must not worry so," she replied with a smile. "You will develop wrinkles, and I have no wish to marry a man who looks older than my father."

"But you shall be careful?" His dark eyes caressed her face. "If the sun sets before we finish our conversation, will you allow Bingley and me to escort you ladies back to Longbourn?"

She nodded as she extended her hand to him, and he bowed over it, kissing her fingers.

When Darcy straightened up and released her, she ran to catch her sister, and her waist-length hair flowed freely behind her. He heard their laughter as they hurried to Longbourn, and he thought it a beautiful sound.

He wanted to hold her abundant curls in his hands and bury his face in them. He longed to touch her face with his fingertips, kiss her tenderly, hear her sigh, breath in her scent, make her laugh.

Darcy could deny it no longer.

I love Elizabeth with my whole self, and I will never love another woman the way I love her.

Having gone to his chambers to make himself presentable, Darcy hurried back down the stairs, eager to have his breakfast.

He stopped short at the side table which held the mail.

What is that?

Recognizing the penmanship, the gentleman picked up the sealed note left in the center of the salver.

Who did this?

He held the folded parchment for a moment before he slipped it into his pocket and continued to the dining room.

Bingley was already seated, enjoying his meal.

"Darcy! You left earlier than usual this morning. You knew I intended to ride with you, so I am most put out."

Darcy served himself from the sideboard and sat across from his friend.

"If you persist in being late," he answered evenly, "you cannot expect that I shall wait for you. I have been riding out early enough to be at Oakham Mount just before sunrise in the mornings and sunset in the evenings."

Bingley glanced towards the door. "I shall accompany you this evening, then."

"You must be certain to meet me on time for our ride, as my friend is expecting you to be with me."

"Your 'friend'?" The younger man grinned. "Will your 'friend' be alone?"

"No, but my very dear friend requires that you be there, too." Darcy smiled broadly. "A member of my friend's family will meet us, as well."

"Capital!" Bingley exclaimed. "I shall be in the courtyard on my horse early."

Darcy nodded and ate his eggs while the note in his pocket seemed to take on weight until it felt like a boulder.

What shall I do? If I give her this letter, I may lose her.

He chewed slowly as he thought through the problem.

There is only one course open to me.

After Darcy had handled all his business affairs, the hours dragged by interminably. By mid-day, Darcy was pacing the grounds of Netherfield, thinking of the conversation taking place between Elizabeth and Charlotte Lucas.

What if Miss Lucas refuses to help?

What if Elizabeth is upset and chooses not to walk tonight?

More than anything else, he wished to break the seal and read the note. *Perhaps I should burn it and be done with it.*

He shook his head. *I cannot in good conscience act with so little consideration of the privacy of the two people involved. It would go against every noble feeling.*

His mind began to travel in a different direction.

Why did the note disappear and reappear?

Finally, he thought of a most curious aspect of the mystery.

Who took the note originally, and why did the thief decide to place it back on the salver? Who would stand to gain the most?

The puzzle intrigued him.

The only people who were at Netherfield both when Beckett left and presently are the members of Bingley's family, me, and the servants. I most certainly did not do it, and I cannot think Bingley would have taken the note only to return it. The servants have no apparent motives. In fact, perpetrating such a scheme would cost them their employment, if they were found out. Since they well know that, I think it extremely unlikely they would do so.

Darcy watched the clouds move slowly across the sky as he pondered the mystery.

Only Caroline, Louisa, and Hurst remain under suspicion. Hurst cares nothing about intrigue. He is far too indolent to engage in such chicanery. That leaves Bingley's sisters. Louisa would be a thief only if Caroline wished for her to act in such a way.

Darcy knew without a doubt that Caroline had been pursuing him for as long as he and Bingley had been friends.

She could have replaced the note, hoping Elizabeth would marry Beckett, leaving me to pay my addresses to her, but why would she have taken it in the first place?

He smiled.

She may have decided to marry Beckett herself after she found that he was noble and wealthy. When he did not return, and Bingley and I dined at Longbourn, she likely reversed her course, hoping to thwart any chance of my wedding Elizabeth.

The gentleman sighed as he turned to walk back to the manse.

I must remember that Caroline's deception is a possibility – not a proven fact. To accuse her without proof would be quite wrong.

Darcy and Bingley arrived at Oakham Mount half an hour before sunset and were rewarded for their punctuality by the sight of ladies approaching the bottom of the hill. After the gentlemen dismounted, tying the reins of their horses to a nearby tree, they walked down the incline to meet the ladies.

Once they regained the crest of the slope, Darcy and Elizabeth walked towards the trees, leaving Jane and Bingley to talk a good distance away.

She glanced up at him. "Should we be so far from Jane?"

"We shall stay within sight of your sister and Bingley. Come." He held out his hand to her. "I wish to show you something."

"A surprise?" Her voice held excitement as she put her hand in his. "For me?"

"Yes. For you. For us."

A few steps farther, just beyond a massive oak tree, Elizabeth found his gift – a lovely carved bench, embellished with roses on the sides of the armrests. The seat was strewn with comfortable cushions, and small tables sat on either side.

She stopped short, holding her breath, dropping his hand.

"You do not like it?" he asked as he searched her face.

"'Tis wonderful," she whispered, looking up at him. "No one has ever done such a lovely thing for me before."

He offered her his arm, speaking quietly. "Perhaps no one has ever adored you as I do."

They walked to the bench in silence and sat down.

"Did Miss Lucas visit?" he asked, releasing her arm with reluctance.

"She did," answered Elizabeth, eyes glistening.

Is she trying not to cry?

"She refused?"

Elizabeth smiled, and his heart soared.

"No, indeed. My friend is very happy for me. She said she noticed weeks ago that you looked at me a great deal, so she was pleased to say she was right. Charlotte has agreed to help us."

Darcy attempted to return her smile, but his heart was heavy as he reached into his jacket pocket and pulled out the letter. He held it out to her.

"Yesterday, I told you Beckett left a note for you, but it disappeared. This morning when I returned to Netherfield, I found it on the salver. Someone must have taken it and decided to put it back."

"I do not want it," she said. "I have made up my mind."

"Please take it. I wish for you to read it."

"Why? I told you it would make no difference to me."

He tried to memorize her face at that moment. "If you refuse to read it, you will never know whether or not it would have changed your answer to me."

She took the letter from his hand, placing it in her lap. "I think you wish me to read it for you. Not for me."

Darcy's lips formed a crooked smile. "Perhaps you are right. I have no inclination to wonder throughout our marriage if you would have chosen him rather than me. I will marry you either way; however, I would like to know."

She raised her eyebrows. "You would marry me, even if I said I preferred Mr. Beckett?"

He nodded solemnly. "I would, unless you changed your mind and wished to call off our arrangement."

"Why? You can marry any woman you choose."

She knit her brows, and he longed to smooth the concern from her forehead.

"No," he replied shaking his head. "I love you with my whole heart. I will marry you, or I shall not marry at all."

Elizabeth lowered her eyes, looking at the letter. "Very well. I shall read it, only because you asked me to do so."

"Then I shall meet you here in the morning. The sun is setting; it quickly grows dark. You must return to Longbourn. I shall walk with you until we see the house. Then I will watch until you are safely inside."

"Thank you, sir."

"Thank you?"

"For keeping me safe," she answered, looking up at him.

"I am a selfish being, Miss Elizabeth. 'Tis what I want to do, after all."

I wish to keep you safe for the rest of our lives. I wish to make you mine.

ROBIN HELM

CHAPTER 15

She is more precious than rubies, and all the things you may desire
cannot compare with her.
Proverbs 3:15

As soon as she was back at Longbourn, Elizabeth hurried to the room she shared with Jane, her mind occupied with the missive in her hand. After she closed the door, she leaned back against it, looking at the writing on the front of it, wondering if she would waver in her resolve once she read it.

I do not wish to read it. He broke his promise, and I cannot easily excuse that. He is not who I thought he was. Was I taken in by his beauty and manners? Did I like him because he was handsome, intelligent, and polished?

A few moments later, she took a deep breath, turned the letter over, and broke the seal.

Dear Miss Elizabeth,

I would much prefer to stay at Netherfield and further our friendship, but I am called away on urgent family business which cannot be delayed. I have no choice.

I will return to Hertfordshire as soon as I am able to do so.

Please forgive me for not keeping my word.

Your servant,
Thaddeus Beckett

She read it through over and over again, trying to understand his secrecy. *Could he not have given some explanation other than "urgent family business"? Why could he not have taken a few moments to come to my room and tell me of it in person? Writing the note likely took more time than he would have spent in telling me face-to-face.*

Hearing a light knock at the door, Elizabeth refolded the paper and placed it in her desk drawer.

"Come," she called.

Jane opened the door. "We must change for dinner. Mama said we have to be there, properly attired, in fifteen minutes."

"'Tis your room as much as it is mine. Why did you knock?"

"I saw the paper in your hand and assumed it was a letter from Mr. Darcy. I thought you would rather read it in private. Was I wrong?"

"Not fully," she replied with a sigh. "Yesterday Mr. Darcy told me Mr. Beckett left a note for me at Netherfield. He thought I had received it already, but I corrected his mistaken assumption. When he returned to Netherfield this morning, he found it on the salver. Someone had taken it, only to return it. Mr. Darcy gave it to me at Oakham Mount."

Jane's face showed her concern. "Have you read the note?"

Elizabeth nodded as she retrieved the letter and handed it to Jane.

After quickly scanning it, Jane looked up at her, tilting her head. "What do you make of what he says?"

"I know not what to think. Mr. Beckett was called from my room at Netherfield the day he left, but he promised he would return.

116

He told me to wait for him, and I did – all day. You know the circumstances. I was already compromised by his actions. Leaving me a private letter on the salver where everyone could see it might make matters worse. He has ruined my reputation and made me the subject of gossip, yet I have had no control over any of it. In fact, I seem to be finding out everything about my disgrace after the fact. How could he be so thoughtless?"

Elizabeth's eyes filled with tears.

Jane embraced her, saying, "You are stronger than this. Dry your eyes and go down to dinner with me, for Mama and Papa will ask questions if you do not. Remember, if Papa thinks any stain attaches to you, he will require you to marry at once. Is that what you want?"

"No. I do care for Mr. Darcy a great deal, but I cannot trust myself to be a good judge of any man's character after I was so mistaken in Mr. Beckett. I wish to know him better before I agree to be his wife. Besides, though the letter was left in a public place at Netherfield, no one knows for certain who wrote it except Mr. Beckett, Mr. Darcy, you, and me."

"Very good points," answered Jane, stepping back. "Now let us help each other dress. We must hurry."

Before a quarter hour had passed, both young ladies had entered the dining room and seated themselves.

Dinner conversation centered on the most exciting bit of news heard in the village that day, shared by Kitty and Lydia, the two youngest Bennet daughters.

"Mama, Kitty and I heard that a militia of soldiers will soon arrive in Meryton. Mrs. Long said they would encamp here for the winter. Is that not exciting? A whole camp full of soldiers," Lydia said, ending with a sigh.

"We shall have more than enough partners at balls and assemblies this winter," added Kitty. "Even Mary and Lizzy will dance."

Elizabeth raised a brow. *Even me? The wallflower?*

Mr. Bennet rolled his eyes before he settled his attention on his wife. "Mrs. Bennet, I hope you have a good menu planned for tomorrow evening, for we are to have a visitor."

"My table is never lacking, sir. And who are we to expect?"

He looked in turn at the women of his family. "My cousin, Mr. William Collins, upon whom Longbourn is entailed. He shall be here a fortnight. Be amiable to the parson, ladies, for when I am dead, he may turn all of you out as soon as he pleases."

"Does he come to inspect his inheritance, or is there some other motive for his visit?" asked Mrs. Bennet.

"According to his letter, he hopes to heal the breach between our families and choose a wife from among our daughters," he replied, glancing around the table. "As we have five daughters, he should have no problem. What say you, Jane?"

Mrs. Bennet shook her head. "Jane is much admired by Mr. Bingley. Perhaps Mr. Collins will settle on Lizzy, for she is the next eldest, and, though she is terribly outspoken, she is second only to Jane in beauty. To my knowledge, she has attracted no suitors. Do you not think she would make a fine mistress of Longbourn?"

"Lizzy? Are you interested in wedding our cousin?" asked Mr. Bennet, looking at his daughter with a mischievous smile. "Should you like to marry a parson? Or perhaps you have another groom in mind."

"Give me a month to think on it, Papa," she answered, eyes glittering with merriment. "At the very least, allow me to meet the man before I make a decision."

Perhaps I shall be married to Mr. Darcy within a few weeks. After all, he has already told me he loves me, and I promised to marry him in a month if he could say those words and mean them.

His only answer was to chuckle into his napkin.

"A parson?" giggled Lydia, her brown curls bouncing as she tossed her head. "Lizzy is too cheerful to marry a dour man of the cloth. Mary would be more suited to him than any of the rest of us. She could quote Fordyce's sermons to him and play for church services."

She and Kitty laughed together as Mary frowned. "I have no plans to enter into matrimony. I rather thought I would care for Papa and Mama as they age."

"Nonsense," pronounced Mrs. Bennet sternly, turning to her middle daughter. "I shall have the dressmaker in Meryton make new frocks for you and Lizzy. Your dresses are quite drab, and hers are suddenly too large. I must insist the both of you be a little more fashionable. All of my girls are pretty, and you two should not sit while others dance."

"Mama, that is unnecessary. I can take them in," answered Elizabeth.

"This time I agree with your mother, my dear," said her father, winking at her. "She is right, you know. Both you and Mary are lately looking a bit shabby. I think your recent illness may have contributed to a loss of weight on your part. You hardly eat at all."

He is thinking of my imminent marriage and does not wish to send me to Pemberley wearing ill-fitting clothing.

"And all this walking about you and Jane do both morning and night does nothing to improve the state of your dresses," added her mother. "Jane never wears her nice gowns when she scours the countryside. You must learn to follow her example."

I walk in my two oldest frocks. I wonder what Mr. Darcy thinks of them. He has admired my hair, and he says he adores me, but he has stopped short of calling me beautiful. Perhaps I should take a bit more care with my appearance.

"I shall help you repair the clothes you use for our exercise, Lizzy," added Jane sweetly. "And we will work together to take in your nicer gowns and pelisses."

Elizabeth smiled at her sister. "You are too good to me."

"The matter is settled, then," said Mrs. Bennet. "We shall visit the dressmaker in the village tomorrow. Mrs. Simpson shall be quite busy for the next month."

The following morning, Darcy and Bingley waited at the foot of Oakham Mount for Elizabeth and Jane.

Elizabeth took Darcy's arm and they walked briskly to the top of the hill.

She turned her face up to his. "Will you tell me the truth about something?"

"I have never lied to you before, and I said I would always be honest with you," he answered with good humour. "What would you ask?"

She blushed. "Do you think I look shabby? I walk in my oldest dresses, and my father wishes to buy me new ones."

"I have rarely noticed your apparel at all. I am too enthralled by your sparkling eyes and your curls," he answered, his dark eyes twinkling in merriment. "You must know that I think you the handsomest woman of my acquaintance."

Her blush deepened as she looked down, hiding her expression. "It sounds as if I want compliments, but I truly do not. I only want to be certain you are not ashamed of me. Mama is taking me to the village dressmaker today for more fashionable gowns. Even Papa thinks I am of late ill-dressed."

He cupped the side of her face with his hand, rubbing his thumb lightly across her cheekbone.

"I could never be ashamed of you, Elizabeth. You are beautiful to me, both in your appearance and in your heart. We shall go to London after we wed, if you agree, and my sister and aunt will take you to their modistes and milliners. You shall have whatever you want."

"So, you do agree with Papa," she answered quietly. "I fear I cannot make you happy. I am bookish, not accomplished. I would rather read than play an instrument or sew, and I engage in chess matches with my father while we discuss politics. Your friends and family will not approve of me. You will regret our marriage, and I cannot bear that. You deserve to be happy."

Darcy frowned. "I did not say I thought you were in need of a new wardrobe. I thought you wanted one. Your clothing choices are entirely your own. My sister and aunt would enjoy visiting the shops with you while you become acquainted with one another."

She looked up at him, and he softened his voice.

"Furthermore, I am already aware of your interests. I know that you read a great deal, and I look forward to doing that with you, learning your preferences, discussing literature, authors, and even politics. To find that you play chess does not discourage me. Far from it. We shall challenge each other. Do you think I would prefer an ignorant, scatter-brained wife who thinks of nothing but herself and what she will wear? A woman who would marry me for my wealth and connections? There are plenty of women in Society who fit that description. Had I wanted such a wife, I would have married years ago."

"My mother says I am far too outspoken. Forgive me?"

"No," he answered firmly.

"No? You will not accept my apology?" *I have gone too far*.

"Elizabeth," he whispered, his hands slipping to rest on her shoulders, "please stop berating yourself. You must not denigrate the woman I love. I would not change anything about you. Why do you not believe me?"

"I have been compared to others all my life and been found wanting. Even you did not admire me when you first saw me."

Darcy smiled. "Which is better, my love? To be admired at first sight only to be found wanting upon further acquaintance, or to grow in another person's esteem the better he knows you? You forget you had a very poor opinion of me when you met me originally. I hope I have improved in your estimation since then."

She shook her head, returning his smile. "'Twas not so much that you improved in essentials upon further acquaintance, but rather my knowing you better raised my opinion of you. I think I understand your disposition now. In essentials, I think you remain as you ever were."

He laughed quietly. "My adorable philosopher."

I think she begins to love me. Why will she not admit it? he thought.

CHAPTER 16

His lord said to him, 'Well done, good and faithful servant; you have been faithful over a few things, I will make you ruler over many things. Enter into the joy of your lord.'
Matthew 25:23

Darcy and Bingley were waiting for Elizabeth and Jane a half hour before sunset. As the minutes crawled by, Darcy felt more than a little agitation. Finally, the sun began to dip below the horizon.

Why are they late? Is she ill? He ran a hand through his hair. *What could have happened? She was fine this morning.* His stomach twisted and knotted painfully.

It was nearly dark when he saw Elizabeth and Jane running towards the place they always met. Relief washed over him, instantly followed by a bit of temper.

He strode quickly down the hill to meet his intended bride, determination and righteous indignation fueling his anger.

Bingley was right beside him.

The man is smiling like an idiot. Does he not know that the woman he cares for is risking her very life?

Darcy struggled to maintain his composure, and when he reached Elizabeth, he offered her his arm, but he kept his eyes forward, not looking at her.

He was silent, maintaining his fast pace as they practically ran to the summit.

"Why are you dragging me?" asked Elizabeth, obviously puzzled and somewhat irritated. "If this is to be my greeting, please refrain from meeting me again."

Darcy clenched his jaw. *She broke her promise to me about one thing. What is to keep her from breaking a promise to me about another?*

As soon as they reached the top of Oakham Mount, he dropped his arm to his side as he turned to glower at her.

"You promised me you would not walk after dark. You know how dangerous it is. Indeed, 'tis the very reason you were injured and compromised, bringing about our current situation."

"Our current situation?" she asked. "You could have asked me why I am out after sunset."

He shook his head. "The reason does not matter. You said you would not do this again. I thought your word meant something. I thought I could trust you, but it appears not. Obviously, you do not take your promises as seriously as I do."

She put her hands on her hips. "Let us be clear with one another. Are you saying you take your promises seriously, but I do not? Do you mean that your trust in my word is broken?"

Darcy took a step back, feeling the fury and outrage rolling from her. "About walking after in the darkness, yes."

Elizabeth narrowed her eyes. "If you can believe I purposely broke my pledge in this instance, how can you have confidence I will not renege on other commitments?"

He took a deep breath. *I have gone too far. She is not harmed, after all.* "Your other vow to me is far more important."

"Why would that matter? If I am untrustworthy in small things, would I not be worse with bigger ones?" She raised a brow. "I believe Reverend Smith gave a sermon on that very subject just last Sunday."

We cannot continue in this manner. I will surely lose her if we do.

Darcy closed his eyes for a moment, forcing himself to calm.

"I was worried about you," he replied softly. "I kept thinking you were injured or ill, or that someone had taken you and your sister. My thoughts were running on so that I feared you had changed your mind."

"Changed my mind? Please, elaborate."

He took a step, reaching for her. She stepped back.

"I thought you might have run away from me." He turned his face away. "After all, I told you I love you, but you did not return those sentiments."

"Had that been the case," she answered, lowering her voice, "I would have told you so myself. I would never break our agreement without telling you. Do you not know me at all?"

Perhaps I should change the direction of the conversation. "Why were you late?"

"You said the reason does not matter," she answered.

He looked at her, unsmiling. "Will you continue to be stubborn, or would you rather resolve this before you must return to Longbourn?"

A full minute passed before she spoke.

"My cousin was to arrive from Kent at four this afternoon, but his carriage suffered a broken wheel, and he did not arrive for several hours after that. My mother held dinner until he was settled. Jane and I could not leave until after we ate."

"And you could not forgo your evening walk?"

Elizabeth glared at him. "I would have forgone the exercise, but I thought you might be anxious if I did not come."

His heart stirred with something akin to joy. "And you did not wish to alarm me?"

"I did not. I knew you would be waiting here, and I thought you would be happy to see me." She sniffed. "It seems I was mistaken."

He took another step towards her, encouraged when she did not back away again. "I am quite pleased to see you. Shall we make a pact not to assume things anymore?"

"Another promise? Will you trust me this time?"

Darcy forced a smile. "I will. Shall we come up with a solution should a similar problem arise in the future?"

"What do you propose?" she asked.

"If you cannot take your walk, tie a handkerchief on the lowest branch of the oak tree just beyond your front gate. If you are not here at the appointed time, I shall ride to Longbourn and look for it. When I see the handkerchief, I will not worry, for I shall know you are safe."

Elizabeth favoured him with a smile, and he felt the iron band around his chest loosen.

"I can manage that," she replied, chuckling. "I used to climb that tree every day when I was a girl."

"Ah! I am secretly engaged to a hoyden," he replied, drawing a laugh from her. "Now, may I escort you to Longbourn? I promise to wait out of sight of your front door."

She nodded, taking his arm as they began to walk in the direction of her home.

He fairly hummed with contentment. "You shall love Pemberley."

"And why is that, Mr. Darcy?" she asked, gesturing with her free hand. "Extensive grounds to explore? Gardens to enjoy? A library that houses the work of generations of Darcys?"

"Why, yes. All of that, as well as thousands of trees to climb."

Elizabeth laughed, and his spirits lifted even further.

As long as I can make her laugh, she will always be mine.

The following morning, Darcy and Bingley again met the sisters at Oakham Mount.

Darcy had hardly slept, thinking back through the disagreement of the prior evening. He realized he had been so upset, he had neglected to question Elizabeth concerning some important information she had related.

After wishing her a good morning, he wasted no time in idle chitchat.

"You mentioned your cousin's arrival last night. Is this the gentleman who will inherit Longbourn one day?"

"It is," she answered.

"I thought he and your father were estranged."

"Mr. Collins is a parson. He wrote to my father, expressing a desire to reconcile."

"That is most commendable," Darcy replied, "but why would your cousin do that after so long an alienation?"

She glanced at the sky, sighing. "My cousin is the parson of Hunsford, and his patroness wishes for him to take a wife. He decided to bring our families together again by marrying one of us."

Darcy felt a sense of foreboding. "Hunsford? Who is his patroness?"

"Lady Catherine de Bourgh of Rosings Park. Have you heard of her?"

"I have. She is my aunt." *And she intends to force a marriage between her daughter and me.*

Elizabeth stared at him. "Your aunt? Your aunt owns the grandiose Rosings Park with sixty-four windows, magnificent staircases – for there are several – multiple ornate fireplaces, shelves in all her closets, and a great deal of beautiful park land? Miss Anne de Bourgh is your cousin?"

He drew in a breath. "I see your cousin has shared his wealth of information."

"Indeed. He has talked incessantly since his arrival. As a result, my mother came to my room last night and demanded that I invite him to join me and my sisters when we walk to Meryton this morning after breakfast."

Darcy's mind whirled with the implications. "Your mother wishes for you to marry your cousin." *Is he handsome? Well-spoken? Intelligent? Pleasant? Will she choose him over me? Does he know of my aunt's expectations concerning my relationship with her daughter?*

She nodded. "She does, for it would ensure she and my unmarried sisters would have a home should my father die. Originally, she thought I was too outspoken to be a parson's wife, but she has changed her mind. My sister Mary does not wish to wed, and my other two sisters would be quite unsuitable wives for a man of the cloth."

"But I would provide a place for them should your father pass prematurely."

Elizabeth shook her head. "My mother does not know that yet. She thinks I have no prospects at all; therefore, I should marry Mr. Collins to secure a future for all of us – myself included."

"This will not do!" he exclaimed. "Can we not announce our betrothal?"

"In two more weeks, if we both can declare our love for one another, I shall agree to a public announcement," she said quietly.

He grasped her hand. "I have already done so."

"But I have not."

His heart stuttered, and he released her. "The original agreement was that you would marry me if I could truthfully say I love you. You said you wished to know me better, but you did not say you must love me."

"That is true," she replied, raising her chin, "but you stated that you wish for a wife who loves you."

He tilted his head as he gazed at her. "'Tis true. I said that. If you feel you cannot love me, tell me now. It would be kinder than leaving me twisting in the wind for a fortnight only to be refused at the end of it."

"Until last night, I did think I loved you, but the idea that you might be constantly angry with me makes me doubt my judgment. I know I can be obstinate and headstrong. Can you love me, in spite of my temper?"

Why does she doubt me? How can I prove what she refuses to believe?

"Did I still love you last night even though we argued? I could have walked away then, but I suggested a solution – a compromise acceptable to both of us. Working out difficulties between a husband and wife is my idea of a good marriage. We shall certainly disagree from time to time, but I will always love you. Do you believe me?"

She bit her lip for a few moments before she spoke again. "I believe you mean what you say right now. Whether those feelings will last is my concern."

He shook his head. *Will she doubt me after we marry? This is not a basis for a good marriage.*

"You have said you thought you loved me until our misunderstanding last night. I have told you my love is constant. I am nothing if not consistent in my feelings, behaviour, opinions, and affections. In fact, every one of my acquaintance knows of my constancy. To be truthful, it bothers me that you can doubt your growing love for me after one minor squabble."

Her expression of extreme sadness broke his heart.

I shall not give up quite yet.

"Where are you going in Meryton this morning? To a shop?" he asked.

She looked up at him.

Is that hope in her eyes?

"We are walking to the dressmaker's shop to have our new gowns fitted."

"Do you mind if I meet you there? I should like to know your cousin." *More importantly, I wish to see the man who would compete with me for your hand.*

"I do not mind at all," she replied gently. "I welcome the opportunity to introduce you to my cousin."

"Very well. I shall see you there."

He took her hand, bowed over it, and turned to walk away. When he reached the top of the peak, he looked back over his shoulder.

Elizabeth stood where he had left her, watching him. She raised her hand, waving at him before she ran to catch up with her sister and continue on her way to Longbourn.

His heart soared. *I was right! She does love me. Now, I must get her to admit it to herself.*

CHAPTER 17

The Lord is my shepherd; I shall not want. He makes me to lie down in green pastures; He leads me beside the still waters. He restores my soul.
Psalm 23: 1-3

Elizabeth tried not to grind her teeth as Mr. Collins prattled on incessantly.

She allowed her mind to drift, nodding occasionally, as she remembered her disagreements with Mr. Darcy. In fact, she had thought of little else in the hours since they had parted, going back in her mind to everything she had said.

When she nearly stumbled over a rock in the pathway, she returned her attention to her cousin. *Mr. Collins is harmless. He is simply boring and somewhat ridiculous. I must not lose my composure; that never turns out well.*

Mr. Darcy's handsome face and imposing figure came to her mind. *Why is it so difficult to believe such a fine gentleman could love me?*

Elizabeth was soon jolted from her reverie by the unctuous tones of her cousin.

"The chimney-piece alone in the small parlour of Rosings cost eight hundred pounds!"

She raised a brow. "It must be a very fine chimney-piece, indeed."

Hearing the whispers and giggles of her two youngest sisters behind her, Elizabeth turned her head to glare them into a more decorous silence.

Jane and Mary led the way, but when Mr. Collins stopped to catch his breath, they turned to face the rest of the party, forming a group perfectly situated for conversation.

"Shall you go with us into the dress shop, sir?" asked Mary, surprising her sisters.

How very odd, thought Elizabeth, quickly schooling her features. *She hardly speaks outside our circle of family and close friends.*

"Of course," he answered, using his black, flat-brimmed hat to fan his pudgy face with one hand while he mopped the sweat from his forehead with a handkerchief held in the other. "Is it not the entire purpose of this journey in the stifling heat?"

"'Tis my purpose as well as Elizabeth's, for we must try on our gowns before we leave the dressmaker's shop. They may need alterations."

Elizabeth detected the worried tone of Mary's voice and saw her unhappy expression. *My sister does not wish for Mr. Collins to be there when she shows us her dresses.*

"Perhaps you might enjoy a trip to the book shop, Mr. Collins, for it is across the street from the dressmaker's," said Elizabeth. "We can join you there after we are done."

His simpering expression turned her stomach.

"I certainly wish to please you, Miss Elizabeth, but I have no need of further books while I visit Longbourn. Your father has a most excellent library, and he has given me leave to borrow freely while I am his guest."

"Shall I go with you to Griffin's then?" asked Jane, smiling placidly. "I have heard they serve ices, and since you have mentioned the extreme heat, I think you would enjoy such a treat. The confectionary is just beside the dressmaker's."

He fluttered his hands and nodded rapidly, his jowls bouncing. "I would indeed, Cousin. I hoped for an opportunity to know you better."

"Lydia and Kitty adore ices," responded Elizabeth. She arched a brow at her younger sisters. "Do you not?" she asked, scowling at them.

Lydia frowned, whining. "But I have spent my pin money, and father said he will give me no more this month."

Elizabeth reached into her reticule and retrieved several coins. "I have yet to spend mine from the past two or three months. Here is enough for both you and Kitty."

"No, Elizabeth," said Mary. She continued in a quiet, solemn voice. "I never use my pin money. I save it to help the less fortunate in our parish. Today, Lydia and Kitty shall be in that category."

While Lydia and Kitty thanked Mary, Jane smirked and looked away.

Elizabeth put her hand over her mouth, barely stopping herself from exploding with laughter.

Who would have guessed it? Mary is a wit. She always seems so severe, but she is kind. Is there more there than I thought? I suppose still waters run deep.

Mary turned slowly before Elizabeth, her reddened cheeks betraying her discomfort.

"You are quite lovely, Mary. The brilliant blue is wonderful with your dark hair and blue eyes."

"But I feel so –" Mary's voice dropped to a hesitant whisper, "– exposed." She tried to pull the bodice of her dress up to her neck.

"My dear sister," said Elizabeth as she walked to stand behind her. "This gown is quite modest. I never realized before what a pleasing figure you possess."

"I cannot wear such a gown to church or out visiting the needy in our village. What reason have I to own such a costly dress?"

"I shall share a secret with you. Jane told me Mr. Bingley is planning to host a ball at Netherfield very soon. He likes the neighbourhood and wishes to establish himself. This gown is perfect for such an occasion. You are beautiful, you know. You should not hide in drab clothing."

"But what of the Apostle Paul's admonition in First Timothy, chapter two, verse nine? 'In like manner also, that the women adorn themselves in modest apparel, with propriety and moderation, not with braided hair or gold or pearls or costly clothing'."

Elizabeth shook her head. "You forget the Apostle Peter's words in First Peter, chapter three, verses three and four. 'Do not let your adornment be merely outward – arranging the hair, wearing gold, or putting on fine apparel – rather let it be the hidden person of the heart, with the incorruptible beauty of a gentle and quiet spirit, which is very precious in the sight of God.'"

"Does that not say the same thing?" Mary's curiosity was genuine.

"The passages do not contradict each other," answered Elizabeth with forbearance, "but the point is that neither passage teaches that women should not wear pretty dresses. The Apostles emphasized inner beauty, moderation, and godliness. The word 'merely' is quite important. We should never be lovely only on the outside, but we can be modest, beautiful, and godly without wearing plain, high-necked, colourless clothing. This gown is quite conservative. Think of the dresses worn by the other women in our circle and compare this gown with those."

Mary rubbed her lower lip with her thumb as she looked at herself in the mirror. "You may be right. You and Jane are physically pleasing without being immodest."

Elizabeth's eyes sparkled. "Thank you, Mary. Will you allow me to arrange your hair? Jane and I would quite enjoy experimenting with different hairstyles for you."

She lifted a hand to her head. "You do not like my hair?"

"On the contrary, dearest," replied Elizabeth, patting her back. "I love your hair. 'Tis so thick and wavy, I have longed to arrange it in a more flattering way for you."

"I have said I have no wish to marry. Why should you go to all this trouble?"

"Because you are my sister, and I love you. You do not seem happy to me. I hope if you look prettier, you will be more pleased with yourself. Would you not like to dance at the ball?"

Mary lowered her head and sighed. "I cannot."

"Have you found a Scripture forbidding dancing?"

"That is not the reason I do not dance."

Elizabeth stepped up beside Mary, placing a finger under her sister's chin to lift it.

"Why, then?"

"I simply cannot. I never learned."

"What? Mama made certain all of us could do the steps."

"You do not remember. I was ill for many of those lessons, and I conveniently left the house for all of the others. I thought no man would ask me to dance, so I never took the trouble to master the art."

"Well!" exclaimed Elizabeth, dropping her hand to her side. "This shall not do at all. Jane and I shall teach you to dance before the ball at Netherfield. Mama was right about this. All of her daughters should be dancing."

"I have no wish to be made light of by Kitty and Lydia. Please forgive me, but I do not want to look ridiculous."

"Look at me, Mary," she coaxed, waiting for her sister's attention before she continued. "Jane and I will teach you privately. I promise no one else will know. We shall not allow anyone to make sport at your expense. Do you trust us?"

Hesitantly, Mary nodded. "I trust you and Jane, but no one else except God."

Elizabeth searched her sister's eyes. *How have I not seen my Mary's unhappiness? Am I that absorbed in my own problems, my own life?*

"Well, then," Elizabeth replied. "Solomon tells us in Ecclesiastes there is 'a time to weep, and a time to laugh; a time to mourn, and a time to dance.' The Netherfield ball will be your time to dance and laugh. I have a great desire to watch you enjoy yourself."

"Very well. I shall do it to please you."

"I hope you will please yourself as well."

The door of the shop opened, and Mr. Darcy entered. His eyes lit with delight. "Why, Miss Mary! How very well you look."

Elizabeth nearly clasped her hands before her. "Is she not quite dazzling?"

Mary turned and fled in embarrassment.

He lowered his voice. "She truly is. Have you heard? Bingley is hosting a ball on Saturday next."

"Jane told me of the ball, but she did not know the date. Next week will be perfect. Mary's gown will surely make her the belle of the occasion."

Darcy lowered his mouth to her ear. "There shall be more than one belle, I think. Are you wearing a new gown?"

She twirled, pleased with his notice. "Do you like it? I have several new dresses."

"Very much. You are even more beautiful than when I saw you last. Is this your choice for the ball?"

"No. I have already chosen another," she teased.

"May I see it?"

"Absolutely not. I wish to surprise you."

"Will you at least tell me the colour?" he wheedled. "I know I shall be stunned into silence at the ball if you refuse to prepare me."

Elizabeth shook her head. "No, and do not attempt to flatter me into changing my mind."

"Shall we trade secrets then? I shall tell you what I plan to wear."

She laughed aloud, rolling her eyes. "Black and white? 'Tis all you own. I am convinced of it."

"Am I so predictable?" He made a show of pouting.

"You have been more unpredictable as of late."

Darcy straightened to his full height. "Which do you prefer? Predictable Darcy or Unpredictable Darcy?"

She sobered. "I wish for you to be yourself all the time. I want to know all your moods. Do you want the same from me?"

"I love you for who you are," he replied in a low voice. "I find you attractive all the time."

She was puzzled. *How can that be? He was angry with me yesterday. How is that love?*

"Even when you think I am unreasonable? Even when I am cross with you?"

His lips twitched. "You possess fire and passion. I have no wish to marry a woman without those qualities. Bingley requires a calm, tranquil lady to match his happy temperament. I would likely be quite unsuitable for a woman such as your sister, as truly wonderful as she is. I am as stubborn as you are, and I can be difficult at times. I know you will never allow me to quench your lively spirit, and I have no desire to do so. You are perfect for me."

"We will argue," she warned.

"And we will reconcile." Darcy chuckled. "I greatly anticipate making up with you after our differences when we are married."

The door flew open, cutting their conversation short, giving Elizabeth no time to puzzle over his words.

Jane approached them. "You must come at once. Lydia and Kitty have met with militia officers, and Mr. Collins is restless. He wishes to return to Longbourn immediately. I think meeting Mr. Darcy might occupy him and stop our sisters from causing a scene."

Mary walked out of the fitting room. "Go, Elizabeth. I shall collect our purchases and join you and the others."

"Shall I not change my clothes first? I have on a new gown," asked Elizabeth, looking at Jane.

Mr. Darcy answered. "The weather is fine, so I think there is no danger of spoiling your gown, though I would rather the officers not see you looking as lovely as you do."

Mary's mouth dropped open, but she rapidly recovered.

Jane smiled knowingly. "Let us go, then."

"Kitty and Lydia will soon make spectacles of themselves, if we do not prevent it." Elizabeth grimaced as she took Darcy's arm and they exited the shop.

Will my family embarrass him? Will he regret our connection?

CHAPTER 18

*Do not go hastily to court; For what will you do in the end, when
your neighbor has put you to shame?*
Proverbs 25:8

Darcy stopped short when he saw the officers gathered around
Elizabeth's younger sisters.

*There are more new officers than I expected. I wonder how
many soldiers are here now. Meryton is overrun, and the two
youngest Miss Bennets are in the middle of it all.*

He soon regained his composure, offering his arm to Elizabeth
and placing his hand over hers in a show of possession. They walked
together to join her sisters and Mr. Collins.

When Mr. Collins turned and opened his mouth, Elizabeth
spoke quickly.

"Mr. Darcy, may I present my cousin, Mr. William Collins? He
has the living at Rosings."

Mr. Collins swept his hat from his head, revealing his sweat-
soaked hair, and bowed so low his shiny forehead nearly hit his
knees.

"So very honoured to make your acquaintance, Mr. Darcy. I am
pleased to say your aunt, Lady Catherine de Bourgh, was very well
the day before yesterday."

Darcy nodded, unsmiling. "My aunt is always in excellent health."

The parson stood, his mouth forming an obsequious smile – which disappeared the moment he noticed Elizabeth's hand in the crook of Darcy's elbow.

He glared at Elizabeth. "Cousin, I should not need to lecture you on proper behaviour with your betters. Lady Catherine would be most put out concerning your familiarity with her nephew, particularly as he is betrothed to her daughter."

Blushing furiously, Elizabeth immediately removed her hand from Darcy's arm and stepped away from the gentleman, joining her sisters with the officers.

Darcy's face darkened. *I would give half my fortune to announce my true engagement at this moment. Would that I had not asked to meet this toadying man, especially since I cannot contradict his statement in public without exposing my aunt for what she truly is – a meddling, overbearing gossip with a propensity to manipulate the truth 'til it is unrecognizable.*

"What?" The gentleman spoke in low tones through clenched teeth. "You assume too much, Mr. Collins. You know nothing of my private life or obligations. In the future, please refrain from commenting on my affairs as they do not concern you in any way. Furthermore, Miss Elizabeth is a gentleman's daughter. As such, she is my equal. You shall not berate her in my presence."

Mr. Collins backed away, nodding his head frantically, his hands clasped in front of his generous paunch.

Darcy turned his attention to the group of officers, seeking Elizabeth. She was smiling in a forced way he had not seen before. He strode to stand beside her, but she did not acknowledge him.

Why are such things so difficult between us? She should have allowed me to announce our betrothal. Does she truly think I would offer for her if I were already betrothed to Anne? Surely, she knows me better than that.

He took several deep, calming breaths. *She is not at fault in this. I must lay the blame squarely where it belongs. This is my doing; I should have told her myself as soon as she mentioned her cousin was my aunt's parson. I will do whatever I must to make it right.*

Darcy glanced around the group of officers, determined to be friendly, but his eyes settled on a man he hoped never to see again. His smile died on his face.

George Wickham – the scoundrel who nearly ruined my sister. He watches Elizabeth and her sisters like a hawk viewing prey. I cannot like the expression in his eyes. The man is insane. I should have encouraged her to change out of that gown when she wanted to do so.

Hearing the sound of distant thunder, Darcy turned his face towards Elizabeth, speaking softly. "I fear rain shall be upon us soon, and it will ruin your lovely gown. That would be a shame, especially as you are wearing a new frock. I would be extremely sorry, for 'twas all my doing. You wished to change, and I discouraged you from doing so. Shall I escort you and your sisters back to Longbourn? If you prefer not to walk, I can hire a carriage from the inn, or we can take shelter in Griffin's. You and Miss Mary did not have ices with the others."

She glanced up at his face, her expression inscrutable. "Mr. Collins is with us. Do you not think him capable of seeing us the short distance to Longbourn?"

He hesitated a moment. *She believes I am betrothed to Anne.* "Of course, your cousin is able to walk back with you, but I should welcome the chance to speak with you a moment. Could you not have two escorts? There are five ladies in your coterie, and you have several packages to carry. I would be happy if you would allow me to be of service."

Her voice was resigned. "Very well. Wait a bit while I gather my sisters and cousin."

Within a few moments, Jane and Mary led the group with Mr. Collins between them. Lydia and Kitty followed, and Elizabeth and Darcy were last in the little procession.

Darcy slowed his gait. Once he and Elizabeth were separated from the rest of her family, he offered her his arm, praying she would accept it.

Instead, she focused her attention straight ahead, studiously avoiding any contact with him.

"What your cousin said is not true," he said quietly. "Anne and I are not engaged. Neither she nor I wish to be married to each other. She is my cousin and my friend, but no more than that."

"Then why would Mr. Collins say such a thing?" she asked, still avoiding any contact with him.

He stopped walking. She took a few steps before she turned to face him.

Darcy cleared his throat. "My aunt and my mother were sisters. Lady Catherine maintains that a marriage between Anne and me was my mother's dearest, heartfelt desire. Supposedly, the sisters planned the union over my cradle."

She lifted her eyes to his. "But you do not wish to marry Anne? Does she consider herself betrothed to you?"

"Absolutely not. Anne has no desire to marry at all. She lacks neither fortune nor consequence and sees me as her brother. Furthermore, *I* definitely do not want to marry a woman whom I view as a sibling. Every feeling revolts."

"But what of your aunt and your mother?"

He frowned. "I have told my aunt on more than one occasion that Anne and I will never marry. She simply refuses to believe I will not obey her dictates. Both my parents are deceased, but they were devoted to one another. I cannot conceive they would choose a loveless marriage for me. Do you believe me?"

She returned to his side. "I do. I have never met your aunt, but from listening to Mr. Collins's rapturous descriptions of her, I warrant she is very capable of reckoning her plans will be obeyed without question."

"Would you have believed me had you not formed a prior opinion of my aunt based on your cousin's ramblings?" *This is the gist of the matter. Will she always require proof of my truthfulness?*

"Why, yes. I think I would have. I have said you are the most honourable man I have ever met. You may omit facts from time to time, but you have never lied to me."

He offered her his arm again, and she accepted it. As they began to walk, he was comfortable once more.

"I have something to tell you, and I hope you will accept it without too many questions," Darcy said, glancing at her. "For this, I would rather not offer proof, although I could."

Elizabeth nodded. "Say what you will."

"I saw a man I know quite well standing among the officers, talking to your two youngest sisters. We grew up together, much like brothers, but he has changed greatly in the past few years and cannot be trusted now. Please do all within your power to make certain your sisters avoid George Wickham. He is no gentleman and would cheerfully ruin them."

She tilted her head, looking up at him. "I shall do what I can. Lydia and Kitty are quite silly, and my mother indulges them."

He smiled down at her. "Is that all? No questions?"

Her eyes twinkled as she shrugged her shoulders. "You will tell me why when you decide to do so. Until then, I have confidence in your judgment."

"He will not hesitate to blacken my character, Elizabeth. When he does so, I shall answer whatever you ask. Wickham is quite the consummate actor – very charming and convincing. He seems to grow worse and worse as time passes. Sometimes, I wonder if he has lost his mind. Please, do not believe him until you talk to me."

"Ah," she answered, chuckling. "Do you trust me?"

"Touché, my love. Of course, I do, but he is quite experienced with the ladies. He knows just what to say."

"You must not worry on my behalf, or you will be old before your time. Besides, I find myself very pleased with my present state. Mr. Wickham cannot influence me against you."

He stopped and took her hand. "Please speak plainly. I dare not hope you are ready to announce our betrothal."

Her smile was sunshine and warmth. "I am, for I now know I love you."

Darcy took a deep breath, feeling as if his heart swelled within his chest. "Will you tell me how long you have loved me?"

"I cannot fix on the hour, or the look, or the words, which laid the foundation. It is too long ago. I was in the middle before I knew I had begun. I fought it with everything within me, but I think I may have begun to fall in love with you when I first met you – even though you most assuredly did not feel the same for me."

He rubbed the top of her hand with his thumb. "You are wrong, you know. I had never before been so bewitched by a woman as I was by you. In fact, 'tis the reason I did not ask you to dance."

Elizabeth raised an eyebrow. "Really? That makes no sense at all."

"Of course, it does," he answered solemnly. "I have been examined like a prize animal at the village fair since I was a thirteen-year-old boy. My friends and relatives have pushed ladies towards me at every opportunity, for a man in possession of a large fortune must be in want of a wife. My attentiveness to any female between the ages of fifteen and forty caused a firestorm of speculation, and I heartily disliked the attention. Had I singled you out at the Assembly, all of Meryton would have had us married by the next morning. Do you understand?"

She narrowed her eyes, pulling her hand away. "I comprehend your meaning, but I cannot forget your words." She put her hands on her hips and mimicked his deep voice. "'She is tolerable, I suppose, but there is rather too much of her to tempt me. She is mistaken if she thinks her handkerchief hides what she is constantly eating. I am not in humour to give consequence to young ladies who are slighted by other men, especially when that slighting is so obviously justified in this case by the lady's lack of discipline.'"

"Good heavens!" he exclaimed in mortification. "I must be careful to think before I speak, for you remember every word. In truth, I did my best not to look at you that evening. I noticed your intelligent eyes, your lovely chocolate curls, and your flawless

144

complexion in a glance, so I searched for a fault. I saw you had a treat in your handkerchief, so I spoke of that to avoid entanglement."

Elizabeth lowered her eyes, looking up at him through her dark lashes. "You know not how those words have tortured me. They ring in my mind."

His cravat seemed to be choking him, and he pulled it away from his neck with one finger. "You are the most beautiful woman I have ever seen, Elizabeth. You must forgive me for what I said then. I am not that man anymore, for you have humbled me. I have loved none but you."

She tipped up her pert nose and sniffed. "I will forgive you if you will do something for me."

"If it is within my power, I will do it," he said, claiming her hand again.

"It is well within your power. There is someone I wish you to meet."

They began to walk once more.

"A family member? Your aunt and uncle in London?" he asked.

Elizabeth smiled widely. "You will certainly meet them in due time, but this is a special friend of mine at Longbourn. She was most unhappy with what you said about me. You must ask her blessing on our marriage and do whatever she requires of you."

Whatever she requires? He swallowed hard. "If I meet her, obtain her blessing, and do what she asks, will you agree to let me announce our engagement?"

Her green eyes sparkled with mischief. "I shall do better than that. My mama will spread the news throughout Meryton before the day is out and begin planning our wedding at once. Are you certain 'tis what you want? After all, you have been studiously avoiding marriage for nearly fifteen years."

"Your mother shall be free to tell anyone she wishes, and I shall put an announcement in the London paper. All I want is for you to be my wife. When shall I meet your friend?"

"Oh, you must meet her today if Mama is to tell the ladies this afternoon. I shall take you to my friend as soon as we arrive at Longbourn," she replied in an airy tone.

Though he could not help being a bit intimidated by the thought of meeting someone so important to Elizabeth, he was ready to do whatever he must to secure her as his own.

CHAPTER 19

And now abide faith, hope, love, these three; but the greatest of these is love.
I Corinthians 3:13

Darcy and Elizabeth were the last of the party to arrive at Longbourn. Instead of entering by the front door, she led him around the house to the servants' entrance.

"Here we are," she said, pausing before the door. "The final labour for my Heracles."

"Have I completed the other eleven without my knowledge?" he asked, smiling.

"You have completed at least twelve with your Herculean efforts to heal my heart after wounding it so thoroughly. This is a special test, never before recorded."

I cannot bear to think of that. I shall make it up to her if it takes my entire life. He resolutely pushed her pain from his mind.

"Why have you chosen Heracles to represent me? For my extraordinary strength and ingenuity?" he teased.

"When I look at you, I do see your strength and ingenuity, but I also see courage, passion, love for children, wit, prowess at games – should I continue, or are you sufficiently puffed up?"

Darcy shook his head, laughing. "My Megara, I have not yet proved my abilities in those areas, but I shall. You see me as better than I am, and I will strive to live up to your good opinion."

"I am to be your Megara? 'Tis a bit disheartening to think you may kill me in a fit of insanity. I do not wish to be your first wife, my hero. I want to be your only wife," she replied.

He grew serious. "I am no hero, Elizabeth. I fear I shall disappoint you."

"You have wrestled my giants and won. You bear the world on your shoulders while you try to keep me safe. You would do anything to protect your friends and relations. What is all that if not an excellent representation of Heracles?" she asked, opening the door to lead him through.

Darcy held the door for her, following her as she stepped into the hallway.

"Elizabeth. Please, wait a moment."

As she turned to him, he drew a small box from his jacket and held it out to her.

"A present? For me?"

"For you, my love," he said. "Before I recovered enough to leave my bed at Netherfield, I sent to London for this. I have carried it in my pocket every day since it arrived, hoping to give it to you should you agree to marry me."

She opened the box and looked up at him tenderly. "This is quite exquisite. I shall always think of you whenever I see it. Thank you," she murmured.

He took the ring from her to slip it on her finger and kept her hand in his.

"A blue sapphire," he whispered. "Since ancient times this gemstone has represented a promise of honesty, loyalty, purity, and trust. The diamonds surrounding the large stone are a symbol of eternal love and desire. According to legend, diamonds were created when bolts of lightning struck rocks, imbuing them with healing powers."

"Perfect," she said smiling. "You are my Heracles, and one of the symbols for your father, Zeus, is a lightning bolt."

Darcy hardly heard her words. She was closer to him than she had ever been before, and her scent filled his mind. He could not think properly.

"My dearest, loveliest Elizabeth. You are so precious to me." Darcy leaned towards her, raising his hands to cup her face, using his thumbs to stroke her cheeks.

She closed her eyes.

He took a deep breath, then drew back abruptly, dropping his hands from her as he exhaled, summoning every ounce of his formidable willpower to rein in his passionate affection for the woman before him.

We must go, or I shall certainly kiss her here in the hallway. I should like for our first kiss to be in a more memorable place, as well as after we announce our betrothal. I am a gentleman. She is a gentleman's daughter and my future wife. Elizabeth will expect better than this. She deserves better.

She tilted her head as she opened her eyes, watching him with evident curiosity.

I shall conquer this and do the right thing – not what I want to do.

He forced himself to peer ahead, clearing his throat. "Shall we find your friend here?"

"This is where she is most likely to be. I spent many pleasant hours in the kitchen with her as a child."

She must be an upper servant, much like my own Nonny. I am already disposed to like this woman who helped to make a happy childhood for my Elizabeth. I just hope she approves of me, despite the abominable way I treated her darling.

Elizabeth peered through the doorway of a small room across from the kitchen. "Mrs. Bailey! I brought someone you must meet."

Before a minute had passed, a kindly-looking lady stood before them, smiling broadly.

"Mr. Darcy, allow me to present our housekeeper and dessert cook, Mrs. Bailey."

She extended her hand, and Darcy took it, bowing. "'Tis my honour to meet you, Mrs. Bailey. Elizabeth has spoken very highly of you."

"Mr. Darcy?" Mrs. Bailey stood tall, holding him with a steady gaze as he straightened to his full height. "Since Lizzy has brought you to me, I must assume she has forgiven you for the humiliation caused by your unkind remarks made in a public place."

I deserved that. "She has been gracious, indeed, to accept my profuse apologies for such inexcusable behavior."

"Mrs. Bailey baked the cookies I was eating at the Assembly," said Elizabeth.

"Cookies?" he asked, glancing from Elizabeth to her friend. "Did you also make the treats Elizabeth brought to Netherfield when her sister and I were ill? Were those cookies?"

Mrs. Bailey smiled, clear blue eyes shining. "Yes, they were. My cookies are Lizzy's favourite sweets, though she limits herself to one each day now. Did you like them?"

"Yes, indeed. I noticed there were several flavours, all quite delicious. One I had never tasted before was particularly good. I think it was some sort of nut."

"Peanuts," she answered. "I brought seeds with me when I moved here from America. It took a bit of experimenting, but I found a way to grow the plants in large tubs my husband built for that very purpose. In the winter, he and the other men haul the tubs into the walled porch which abuts Longbourn's flower and herb gardens. The multiple large windows catch the sunlight, much like a conservatory."

His deep brown eyes sparkled with interest. "I should love to have you come to Pemberley and instruct my gardeners on your method. I designed and oversaw the building of a large conservatory adjoining the back of the house for growing plants and fruit trees all year round. Three large fireplaces built into the wall heat the building in winter. Perhaps you could also give my housekeeper your recipes, if you like. When Elizabeth is the mistress there, she will still require her cookie each day."

"So, you are the man who stole my girl's heart? You will take her away to Derbyshire?"

Elizabeth put her hand on Mrs. Bailey's arm. "I would have told you earlier, but I accepted his proposal less than an hour ago."

Mrs. Bailey's grave expression showed her concern. "Are you certain about this, Lizzy? Once 'tis announced, you cannot change your mind without bringing censure to your name as well as his."

"My acceptance was provisional," said Elizabeth, chuckling a bit. "He has to receive your blessing on the marriage, and he must do whatever you ask. We have yet to tell my parents or sisters, though my father has known for a while that a betrothal was imminent. I have also confided in Jane and Charlotte, though I have not yet told them I accepted."

Mrs. Bailey turned her eyes to Mr. Darcy. She spoke softly. "Do you truly love her? Can you accept her for who she is?"

He thought of the pain his careless remarks had caused Elizabeth, and he fought the tears gathering in his eyes. "I love her with all my heart, and I will never knowingly hurt her again. There will be no other woman for me."

The housekeeper then focused on Elizabeth. "Are you sure you love him, my dear? He is handsome and wealthy, to be sure, but does being with him make you happy?"

Elizabeth smiled. "He has pursued me and loved me in a way that I would never have expected. He is as constant as the sun. We are well-matched in temperament, interests, and expectations. Indeed, I am happy beyond my wildest expectations to be marrying a man whom I love so well, and I fear no other man could compare to my betrothed."

Mrs. Bailey smiled through tear-filled eyes. "Then you both have my blessing. I shall make you a wedding breakfast that shall be remembered and talked of in Meryton for years, and Longbourn will shine as it never has before."

"Thank you," Darcy said, pulling Elizabeth to his side. "Now, dear lady, what do you ask of me?"

"You owe me nothing, Mr. Darcy."

"Perhaps not, but I would hear your request, if you will. You are important to my future wife; therefore, you are important to me."

The older lady nodded. "My husband and I have already spoken of what we would do when our dear girl marries, and we would like to go with her to her new home. We have no children, but Lizzy has filled that emptiness in our hearts, and we wish to be where she is."

"You and your husband are welcome to visit Pemberley at any time of your choosing, Mrs. Bailey. You will always have an open invitation to be our guests."

She shook her head. "We do not ask to be your guests. Indeed, that would make us quite uncomfortable."

His confusion was evident. "We already have an excellent housekeeper at Pemberley, Mrs. Bailey, and she has been with us since I was a boy. I doubt Mrs. Reynolds would want to give up her position, and I cannot ask it of her."

Mrs. Bailey laughed. "I imagine you are correct, Mr. Darcy, and I would not dream of displacing her or anyone else. In fact, I have no desire to manage a household the size of yours. I would rather confine myself to making sweets, if your cook is amenable to sharing her kitchen. I have an idea of how to use icing to decorate cookies which I would like to explore, and I have been thinking of making small cakes instead of large ones. I have already planned a frosted wedding cake for my Lizzy's wedding breakfast, though I had no idea it would be required so soon.

"My husband and I wish to experiment with growing vegetables, fruits, and other plants, like peanuts, throughout the year. His tremendous knowledge of horses could help you, and when your children come, we would love to help care for them. Do you have any use for an older married couple who wish to experiment with what interests them?"

My Nonny died several years ago. Mrs. Bailey reminds me of her a great deal. She seems quite excited about her plans. Darcy turned his eyes to Elizabeth, noting the happiness she exuded. *She would have family at Pemberley. When I am gone during the day, Mr. and Mrs. Bailey would be there for her. I would not worry every minute when we are apart as I do now. She would putter in the gardens with them rather than walking the grounds alone, and my mind would be at ease. Their presence would make me a better master.*

He nodded to Mrs. Bailey. "I think your ideas are wonderful. I know Elizabeth would be more comfortable at Pemberley if you and your husband were there, and anything that can add to my future wife's happiness is important to me. Normally, I am not so forward with ladies, Mrs. Bailey, but as this is a business agreement, shall we shake hands?"

When he offered his hand, she chuckled and accepted the gesture, glancing at Elizabeth.

"I quite like your young man, Lizzy. He will do very well for you."

After a short meeting with a most genial Mr. Bennet, the young couple made their way to the parlour to share the joyous news with the rest of the Bennet family.

However, the announcement was forestalled.

By the fireplace stood a tall, golden-haired man.

Thaddeus Beckett had returned, thwarting Darcy yet again.

CHAPTER 20

He raised Himself up and said to them, 'Who is without sin among you, let him throw a stone at her first.'
John 8:7

Elizabeth stood frozen in place, eyes wide. *Why is he here?*

Her mother and two youngest sisters sat silently in the room, watching the scene with undisguised interest.

Jane's gaze was focused on her needlework while Mary stared at her book and Mr. Bingley peered out the window.

Beckett stepped forward and bowed. "Darcy. Miss Elizabeth."

Darcy, unsmiling, returned the gesture. "Beckett."

Elizabeth, regaining her equilibrium, nodded to the physician. "Mr. Beckett."

"I should very much like to speak privately with you, if you would grant me the honour," Beckett said quietly, his blue eyes pleading with her.

She glanced up at Darcy, her voice low. "Do you mind? We shall stay within your sight, if you agree. Of course, if you object, I shall refuse his request."

"I trust you completely, and to a lesser degree, him," replied the gentleman. "A conversation between the two of you may set his mind, and yours, at rest. I think we all would prefer that the matter be settled."

"Thank you for trusting me," she murmured.

He rose even further in her estimation. *Very few men would extend such courtesy to a man who has compromised his fiancée three times.*

Beckett signaled for her to lead the way, so she guided them to the gardens, stopping at a bench to sit.

The younger gentleman sat beside her, but Darcy walked a short distance further and turned to face them, arms folded across his chest, expression dispassionate.

"Did you receive my note?" asked the physician, drawing his brows together.

She fixed a level gaze upon his angelic face, his blond hair a nimbus in the sunlight.

The hubris of the man! "I did. You left it in a public place, and Mr. Darcy saw it. The letter disappeared for a bit, but then he found it again. He brought it to me, though it was improper for you to write me. Surely you knew you were exposing me to further gossip."

He drew in a deep breath and stood, hands clasped behind his back. "You are right, of course. I have behaved most thoughtlessly where you are concerned. I assure you, I do not usually act so rashly. I must beg your pardon. Please forgive me."

Elizabeth also rose to her feet, head held high. "You are forgiven. Though you placed me in a precarious position, I am unharmed. Is that all you wished to say?"

"I came to tell you why I left, as well as why I have been so long delayed in returning."

"That is unnecessary, Mr. Beckett," she said firmly. "We are polite acquaintances. You helped me in a professional capacity, and I appreciate all you did for me. You owe me nothing."

He groaned. "I wish to be more than a polite acquaintance."

When she made no response, he continued. "My parents' carriage had overturned and rolled down an embankment, but the circumstances were such that it may have been a planned attack on their lives. They were both badly injured. Indeed, their coachman died from his wounds, and it was questionable whether they would survive the night or not. I had no choice but to leave immediately, for I was summoned as their son, as well as their physician."

She put a hand to her mouth. *I have misjudged him.* "I know not what to say. I am so sorry for your pain and their suffering. Have they recovered?"

Beckett shook his head, his expression infinitely sad. "My father has improved, but my mother may never fully regain use of her legs. I would have come to you that day, but I knew I would be unable to keep from telling you everything if I saw you. 'Tis why I wrote instead."

Her voice was gentle, compassionate. "Why was there a need for secrecy?"

"I already told you my father is the Duke of Ormonde. What I did not say is he is in the direct line to inherit the throne, though the king has fifteen children who would be crowned before my father. Even so, my father is one of His Majesty's closest advisors. No information is ever released concerning those in the king's inner circle unless he first gives permission. His Majesty chose to withhold his consent until after an investigation into the incident could be conducted. Even now, we are limited as to how much information we may impart."

"I understand. You had no choice." Her tone was sympathetic.

"Please, tell me I am not too late," he said, taking a step closer to her.

"Too late?"

His eyes searched her face. "I came back here for you. I wish to pay my addresses, to know you better, to convince you I could be a good husband to you."

She lowered her gaze. "I am betrothed to Mr. Darcy."

"I know you felt something for me, as I did for you. I still do," he said, imploring her.

Elizabeth raised her face to his. "At one time, I did believe I could love you, but I realize now I may have been charmed by the idea of you – a handsome, intelligent, kind man who paid marked attention to me. I could tell you admired me, and that was flattering – a novelty."

He clenched his fists by his sides. "Do you love him?"

"I do. I would not marry him otherwise." She spoke persuasively. "There is no lack of eligible ladies, Mr. Beckett. You shall have no difficulty in fixing your affections elsewhere, and those feelings will be returned."

A frown marred his beautiful countenance. "I have yet to feel for any other lady what I feel for you. Do not dismiss my love so lightly, as if I am capricious."

Beckett turned his face away. "My heart is broken. Perhaps I shall not marry at all," he muttered under his breath.

"You feel that way now, but you will soon forget me."

"Would that I could. I fear I shall not erase you from my mind as quickly as you abandoned all thoughts of me."

She shook her head and reached towards him. "Come, shake my hand. I have lost neither the memories of how you helped me when I was injured, nor the way you cared for my sister during her illness. Let us be friends with no acrimony between us. Shall we agree to remember the past only as it gives us pleasure?"

He accepted her hand, bowing over it. "I sincerely wish you all joy, and I hope that Darcy will endeavour to deserve you. If you ever need me, I shall be at your disposal."

Darcy's voice sounded from behind him. "Thank you for your good wishes, Beckett. Be comforted, for I will always do my best to make my wife happy, though I doubt I shall ever truly deserve her," he said, walking to her side.

"Now, should I seek out a new physician," Darcy continued, "or are you able to get past your disappointment and continue to be the physician for my family?"

Beckett straightened up and turned to face Darcy. "Are you certain you can trust me with your wife?"

Darcy smiled benignly. "No, but I am quite positive I can trust my wife with you, for she has more honour than either of us. I also know that you shall make her well-being a priority, and that is what I want – an excellent physician who seeks the best for my beloved. Can you do it?"

Beckett gave a sharp nod of his head. "I take my profession quite seriously. I always seek what is most effective for my patients. Now, I take my leave of you, for I must return to London. Good day to both of you. Best wishes for a long and happy life together."

He turned on his heel, striding quickly towards his carriage which awaited him in front of Longbourn. As soon as he was seated inside, he rapped on the ceiling and was on his way.

Darcy offered Elizabeth his arm. "Shall we make our announcement now? I confess, I was a little disappointed to have to wait."

She tucked her hand into the crook of his elbow. "Prepare yourself for a great deal of enthusiasm. In all likelihood, an embarrassing display of excitement awaits you."

He chuckled, pulling her closer to his side. "As there will be a distinct lack of enthusiasm from certain quarters of my family, I think I can bear a bit from your mother and sisters. By the way, would you be happy to wed in three weeks after the banns are read? Would you rather wed sooner than that? I should be quite pleased to go to London for a special license and marry you Saturday."

Elizabeth smiled as she glanced up at him. "My mother would likely faint dead away if we were to have our wedding sooner than three weeks. There are clothes to buy, a breakfast to plan, things to do!"

"I was thinking of a small, private ceremony limited to our immediate families."

She laughed aloud. "Then you may wish to reconsider marrying me, for the first wedding in the Bennet family will surely take place in front of the full population of Meryton society – four-and-twenty families – as well as my relations and yours. I am sorry to pain you, but it cannot be avoided. Can you bear it, my love?"

"I can bear a great deal more than that to be your husband," he answered, his dark eyes alight. "That was the first time you called me your love. While I bask in the glow of this moment, lead me to your family, for I am quite ready to face them all."

Darcy and Elizabeth stood in front of her family and Mr. Bingley, meeting their expectant stares together. He took her hand in his, clearing his throat as everyone quieted.

"Elizabeth has agreed to be my wife, and all that remains is for us to set a date."

The words had barely left his mouth when Mrs. Bennet was out of her seat, hugging her daughter with effusions too numerous to mention.

Once the cacophony had subsided a bit, he calmed himself and tried yet again.

"We must set a date for the wedding. I prefer to marry as soon as possible and return to Pemberley, for I have been away from my estate business far too long."

Mrs. Bennet nodded. "Yes, indeed. We shall have the banns read for the next three Sundays, and you may wed the following Friday or Saturday, three weeks from now."

He answered quickly. "Today is Friday. If the banns are read Sunday, we can marry two weeks from Monday. As an alternative, I can go to London and obtain a special license to wed without the reading of the banns. We could marry two weeks from today."

"Two weeks?" She blanched, sitting down and taking a breath. "But we have so much to prepare – her wedding clothes, the breakfast, invitations to our extended family. Should you not like your family to be present, as well? They must make plans to travel here."

"My sister will come, of course," he answered, "and my Fitzwilliam relatives. I shall invite my aunt and her daughter, but I doubt they will attend."

Collins stood, clearly agitated. "Her ladyship will be most displeased, and as she is my noble patroness, I shall not be present either. In fact, I have decided to leave Longbourn immediately. I received an invitation just this morning to dine at Lucas Lodge tonight, and I believe I must accept their generous offer. Perhaps they will allow me to stay with them until I can arrange transportation back to Hunsford."

He bowed and nearly ran from the room.

"Well, he has no reason to be in a huff just because Lizzy prefers Mr. Darcy to him. Who would not?" Lydia giggled and Kitty joined her, wagging their eyebrows. "Um-mm."

Elizabeth and Jane blushed, but Mary frowned at her youngest sisters. "It behooves us all to be charitable to those who are – less fortunate in appearance or circumstance. Mr. Collins is our cousin and a parson. He deserves our respectful compassion. Kindly restrain yourself from making sport of him, for he is suffering enough at this moment. In coming here, he was trying to do what he thought was right."

Lydia and Kitty rolled their eyes, smirking.

Elizabeth bit her lower lip. "Thank you, dearest Mary. Now, about the date. Mr. Darcy has so many people who depend upon him. Surely two weeks is sufficient time. Jane and I will help you, Mama, and so will Mrs. Bailey, even though she and Mr. Bailey will be preparing to move to Pemberley as well."

For once, Mr. and Mrs. Bennet spoke as one. "What?"

"They have not spoken with you concerning their request to move with Elizabeth to Pemberley?" Darcy asked, tugging on his cravat, clearly uncomfortable.

Mr. Bennet shook his head. "They have not, but I should not be surprised. When Elizabeth had her nineteenth birthday, Mrs. Bailey came to me and requested that we employ a young lady of her choosing. She said she would like to retire when Elizabeth married. I agreed, and before much time had passed, she presented her niece, lately come from America. She has been training the young woman to be a housekeeper since then."

Mrs. Bennet made a sound very like, "Humph!" Then she added, "Has Mrs. Bailey taught her niece to make her desserts, as well? For every woman in Hertfordshire with a household to run has been trying to lure her away from Longbourn for her recipes. They are happy enough with their housekeepers. Lizzy, you have been most high-handed to steal her from us."

Elizabeth noticed Darcy's frown and spoke quickly in conciliatory tones. "Mama, I had no intention of stealing Mrs. Bailey. She asked us if she and Mr. Bailey could come to Pemberley with us. Mr. Darcy graciously granted her request. Surely, you would not have her stay here when she and her husband wish to go with us. We shall provide for them when they are too old to work. Are you able and willing to do that?"

Mr. Bennet nodded slowly. "As you know, we are in no position to provide for our servants once I depart this earth. Indeed, Lizzy, should your mother and unmarried sisters outlive me, they will depend upon the kindness of you and your husband themselves. Mr. and Mrs. Bailey have served us well for many years. I am happy to think they shall never have to worry about what will happen to them in their old age."

Darcy squeezed Elizabeth's hand. "I have already thought of that, sir. I intend to refurbish the dower house at Pemberley. It will be at your family's disposal should they need it."

Mr. Bennet looked at his wife pointedly. "My dear?"

She sighed. "Oh, well. If you put it that way, I suppose I must allow it to be so." She turned her attention to Elizabeth. "Will you ask her to leave her recipes for her niece?"

"Of course, Mama. I imagine she has already been teaching Janalyn to bake, but I will make certain she has the recipes for your favourite sweets."

Darcy cleared his throat again. "The date?"

"The dower house at Pemberley," said Mrs. Bennet on a sigh. "I would never have thought things could end in this happy way."

Mr. Bennet grimaced. "The date, my dear. Please, try to attend. The date for the wedding must be agreed upon."

Mrs. Bennet's eyes gleamed. "A special license? How well that sounds. Yes, Mr. Darcy. Two weeks from today will do very well. I shall write immediately to my brother Gardiner in London to inform him of our plans. After I run an errand or two in Meryton, of course."

Mr. Bennet winked at Elizabeth. "Shall I send for the carriage?"

"Oh, yes, my dear, at once!" answered his wife. "There is no time to waste. I shall be back in time for dinner. Mr. Darcy, you and Mr. Bingley must stay and eat with us. Mary, please advise Mrs. Bailey there will be guests."

Mr. Bingley stood. "Mr. Bennet, may I request an audience with you?"

The elder gentleman chuckled. "Of course. My library has been quite well-used as of late. Perhaps I should install a door which does not lock. A simple push would be so much quicker."

Elizabeth looked at Jane, very happy to acknowledge her with a small inclination of her head.

When Mr. Bingley and Mr. Bennet left the room, Elizabeth took advantage of the chattering between her mother and two youngest sisters, standing on her tiptoes to whisper into her fiancé's ear.

"Double wedding?"

"Shall your mother survive it?" he asked in an undertone.

"She has lived for this since we were born, you know."

"Then Bingley shall have to go with me to London."

Elizabeth giggled. "Two special licenses? She may die of happiness."

"Ah! Two weddings and a funeral," he deadpanned. "Better than two special licenses."

Jane and Mary joined in the laughter until the three elder sisters were crying, hugging one another.

He watched their display of familial joy and grinned. "Georgiana shall have a sister in two weeks. She will be overjoyed."

Elizabeth glanced back at him. "She will have five sisters, and we will love her."

Darcy's smile suddenly melted from his face.

She looked up at him. "Whatever is the matter?"

He shook his head. "We must talk."

CHAPTER 21

And why do you look at the speck in your brother's eye, but do not consider the plank in your own eye? Or how can you say to your brother, 'Let me remove the speck from your eye'; and look, a plank is in your own eye? Hypocrite! First remove the plank from your own eye, and then you will see clearly to remove the speck from your brother's eye.
Matthew 7:3-5

Darcy followed Elizabeth to the small wilderness just beyond the gardens of Longbourn. She sat on a stone bench and gestured for him to join her.

He sat beside her, his stiff posture revealing his agitation.

"You wished to speak privately?" she asked.

"I would rather not talk of these matters, but it must be done."

How shall I do this without offending her? he pondered. *Perhaps 'tis better to start with the log in my own family's eye rather than the mote in hers.*

He stood and began to pace, hands clasped behind his back.

After a few moments, he stopped to face her.

"The better I know your sister Jane, the more I like her."

Elizabeth's confusion was apparent. "I cannot imagine anyone would dislike Jane."

"She puts me in mind of my own sister, Georgiana, though Miss Bennet is her elder by six or seven years."

"Miss Darcy is reserved?"

"Yes," answered Darcy, pleased by her response. "She is quiet – even shy."

Elizabeth waited in silence.

How can I say this without portraying Georgiana in a very poor light? Elizabeth has yet to meet her. I would not prejudice her before she can form her own opinion.

She stood and placed her hand on his arm. "Something troubles you, my love. Share the burden with me."

He swallowed. "I told you earlier that I recognized George Wickham in Meryton with the other officers, and I said he cannot be trusted. After observing the friendliness of your younger sisters, I am convinced I must lay a most distressing story before you to make you understand what a libertine and wastrel he truly is.

"I have known him all my life. His father, an excellent man, was my father's estate manager. He married a good woman soon after my father wed my mother. Wickham and I were born within months of each other. He was my father's godson, and we were inseparable for many years. In fact, my father, in order to secure a good future for his godson, paid for his studies in college and at Cambridge. He was given every opportunity to do well. His education provided him with the ability to enter religious orders, and my father granted him the living at Kympton.

"After my father died, Wickham informed me he had no desire to take orders. He was no saint, but I had no idea he had sunk so low. He asked for a final settlement of £3,000. I gladly gave him the money, for he had changed so much I felt he was not fit for the clergy. Sadly, he squandered the money, living a life of dissolution."

Elizabeth gasped, covering her mouth with her hand. "Oh, how beastly! He has ruined his chances of a good life."

Darcy continued. "Exactly so, and it appears he plans to take as many people down with him as possible. He hates me and does all that he can to thwart me."

"Why would he hate you? You gave him the money he wanted."

"Once he had spent all he had, he came to me again, but I refused to continue to fund his debauchery. Wickham seemed almost wild when I denied his plea, then sought to retaliate against my family by destroying my sister's reputation."

"Such wickedness," she muttered, gaping at him.

He resumed his story. "Last year, Georgiana and her companion, Mrs. Younge, went to stay in Ramsgate for the summer. Wickham, now known to be friends with Mrs. Younge, followed them there to seduce my sister, hoping to elope with her, thereby gaining control of her £30,000 dowry. She was but fifteen years old at that time. Even I would never have thought him capable of such wickedness. I wondered if he had lost his mind entirely."

"My sister Lydia's age."

"Exactly so," he answered, watching her closely. "Young ladies are easily influenced by his handsome face and deviously charming ways."

Elizabeth was quiet for a moment. "How was Wickham thwarted?"

"I went to visit Georgiana in Ramsgate and, by chance, happened upon them together. She confessed the entire scheme to me. When next I saw Wickham, he was crazed. Though he threatened me with violence, I immediately dismissed Mrs. Younge and took my sister back to Pemberley. I have told no one, except you and my cousin Colonel Fitzwilliam, for fear of damaging her reputation irreparably. I trust you will guard this information."

"You may be assured of my secrecy," she answered. "I am honoured to be in your confidence, but I wonder, why tell me about this right now? Could it not have waited until tomorrow?"

Darcy took her hand in his. "In two weeks, your sisters will be my sisters. Wickham resents me, and he may seek to hurt me by ruining one of them. Miss Bennet will be soon married, and Miss Mary would not be taken in by a rogue. However –"

She interrupted him. "You think Wickham will seek to despoil Kitty or Lydia? My father has no money to give him, so Wickham would attempt to blackmail you?"

"He would. Wickham has sunk to the depths of depravity. I have never seen anything else like it. He lost all sense of propriety. Nothing is beneath him; he would stoop to the lowest acts to hurt me. His revenge would be complete. Apart from that, I would be most unhappy to be the cause of suffering befalling any member of our families."

She nodded soberly. "I shall speak with Papa and Jane of your concerns. My father will make certain Mr. Wickham will not be welcomed at Longbourn."

"That may not be enough, my love," he said, releasing her hand, lifting his fingers to her cheeks. "Your sisters might still meet with the scoundrel in Meryton. You and I will be gone in a fortnight. Miss Bennet probably will remove to Netherfield at the same time, for I would not be surprised to hear of her betrothal to my friend when we return to the house, and I suspect they will wed when we do. Who will go to the village with your youngest sisters? Who will protect them?"

Her eyes filled with tears. "I do not know."

"Shall we take them with us to Pemberley until the militia leaves Meryton?"

"You would do that for me?"

He gently wiped her tears with his thumbs. "Do you not understand? I love and adore you with all my heart. I would do anything to spare you pain."

Her gaze softened. "I love you, too. While I am pleased that you would welcome my sisters, we will be newly married, and I wish to have you to myself for a few weeks, at least." She blushed and lowered her eyes.

She desires to be alone with me? Darcy was a happy man. "I am glad to hear you say that, for to confess the truth, I would rather not share you with others for a good while after we wed. We could take a wedding trip after I finish my business on the estate. Would you like that?"

"Very much," she answered, looking up at him with sparkling eyes. "Perhaps we can take them to London to visit with my Aunt and Uncle Gardiner. Mary could stay here so Mama would not be deprived of all her daughters at one time."

Her face was so close to his. Before he could weigh his actions, he moved his hands to the back of her head, drawing her even closer. Her eyes drifted shut, and he forced himself to be as gentle as a whisper.

Darcy's lips barely touched hers. He tilted his head, delighted to breathe in her scent and feel her hair under his fingers. When he sensed her arms reaching around him, her small hands moving against his shoulder blades pulling him closer, his control began to slip.

This must stop. Anyone could walk by and see us. Darcy, summoning all his willpower, broke the kiss, leaning his forehead to hers.

"I must apologize," she said quietly, stepping back, lifting her palms to her cheeks, closing her eyes.

"*You* are sorry? For what?"

"I touched you, and I should not have. I shall be more careful in the future." She blushed deeply in mortification.

His voice was low. "Elizabeth, look at me. Are you under the impression that what you did was improper? Did I seem displeased to you?"

"You stopped when I did not wish to do so. I must have done something wrong." Her green eyes glistened with tears.

Darcy shook his head. "Impossible. You responded to me exactly as I have dreamed you would. Pray, do not distress yourself."

"Then why did you stop?" Her lips trembled. "Did you not like it? Surely, I shall improve with practice."

He raised both eyebrows, chuckling. "What a marvelous idea, my darling girl. We shall practice a great deal – *after* we are married. I stopped because I truly did not want to do so."

169

She widened her eyes. "So, I did not do it badly? I have never before kissed a man in such a way. I do not know how to do it well."

His heart seemed to swell within his chest. *Beckett did not kiss her.* "You have bestowed on me a wonderful gift, for you will never compare my kisses to those of another man, and we can show each other what we enjoy."

Elizabeth beamed at him. "You have given me so much already. I am quite happy that I am able to gratify you with my lack of experience. Shocked, really. I thought I would disappoint you, and you might turn away. Mama said we must please our husbands, or they would look elsewhere for their pleasure. I have been anxious about it."

Darcy could not help himself. He was beyond curious, and it seemed to him that she was not uncomfortable talking about it. "I worried that I would frighten you. Did you like it?"

She laughed. "Could you not tell? I embarrassed myself by trying to draw you closer." She paused. "What did you mean that you stopped because you did not want to? You wanted to continue to kiss me?"

"You are so delightfully curious. I wondered if you heard that."

"Of course, I heard it. I always listen to you. Answer the question, sir," she teased.

"I wanted to keep kissing you, and I knew we might be seen," he answered, taking both her hands in his. "I would not wish our display of tenderness to be fodder for gossip. Evidence of our devotion for one another is too precious to display before people who would demean you. In addition, kissing you makes me want to be even more affectionate, and that must wait until after our vows."

"More affectionate?"

He rubbed his thumbs lightly over the backs of her hands. *She is an innocent, but I will not discourage her from talking to me. I will always answer her questions. Heaven knows I would rather educate her on such matters rather than allowing her mother to frighten her further.*

"Yes, my love. Why did you pull me to yourself?" he asked.

"I have never had such strong feelings for a man before, and I did not know how to properly express my love for you."

Darcy smiled. "And I have loved no other woman in the way I love you. There are many ways to show our love, and we will explore those together, *after* we wed."

"No more kisses for a fortnight?" she pouted.

"I cannot promise that, but I will do my best. Perhaps we should try not to be alone in such a private place again until the conclusion of the ceremony."

Elizabeth sighed. "The next two weeks shall seem very long indeed."

With a special license, we can wed whenever we choose. He tried to clear his mind of the thought. *Her mother would never forgive me, and Elizabeth deserves a wedding day. If I stay very busy, the time shall pass more quickly.*

With a smile, he released her hands and offered her his arm. As they began to walk to the house, he patted her fingers, tucked in the crook of his elbow.

"We shall be quite occupied, sweetling, preparing for our wedding. I must go to London tomorrow to complete several items of business, and you should begin packing a trunk of what you shall need as we travel after we wed. I shall arrange to have the rest of your belongings collected and taken to Pemberley. Mr. and Mrs. Bailey can make their journey in that carriage with your trunks. They shall likely arrive at Pemberley before us."

She sighed. "I suppose you are right, dearest, though I shall miss you most dreadfully until you return. I fear you have become necessary to my happiness."

"Then, as your mother invited me, I shall dine at Longbourn this evening to see you one last time before I leave. Doing so will lessen the time we spend apart. However, if you need me, you have only to send an express to our home in Town. 'Tis not that far away. I shall write down the direction for you before I leave."

"Now, if I can simply arrange an emergency of some sort to bring you back to me," she chuckled, looking up at him.

You have no idea of the depth of my feelings. Nothing could keep me away a minute longer than absolutely necessary.

CHAPTER 22

Satan himself transforms himself into an angel of light.
II Corinthians 11:14

Elizabeth was quite pleased to be distracted from the melancholy she felt due to Darcy's absence when her elder sister and Mr. Bingley announced their engagement a quarter hour later.

Amidst the confusion of congratulations, she pulled Jane aside, drawing her into an embrace. "Fitzwilliam told me before he left that he expected an agreement between the two of you. I am beyond pleased for you, Jane, for I think you both shall be very happy."

Jane smiled, blushing prettily and stepping back to reply. "I am truly overjoyed. I only wish everyone could be as fortunate as we are."

"When do you plan to wed? Have you spoken of it with Mr. Bingley?"

"Charles hopes that you and Mr. Darcy will agree to a double wedding. He will leave for Netherfield within the hour to speak with your betrothed, hoping that the two of them will journey to London together and secure special licenses."

Elizabeth hugged her. "Rest assured, there shall be no objections on our part, for we have already spoken of sharing our wedding day with you. How wonderful to know that we shall be giving great pleasure to all our relations! Sisters and best friends marrying in the same ceremony must be agreeable to everyone."

As soon as Mr. Bingley left Longbourn, Mr. Bennet retired to his library, citing extreme fatigue.

Mrs. Bennet, accompanied by four of her daughters, set off for Meryton to spread the joyful news and commission wedding dresses for Jane and Elizabeth.

As Mary had several gowns she had yet to wear, she elected to remain at home, pleading a headache.

Kitty and Lydia had groused the entire time they were in the carriage, insisting they needed new gowns for the wedding as much as the brides did. Mrs. Bennet agreed, for she never denied them anything, so the two youngest Bennets fled the carriage as soon as they arrived at the dressmaker's shop, stating their determination to be assisted before the brides.

Their underlying strategy soon became evident, for immediately after the two of them had selected their fabrics and chosen designs for their dresses, they left the shop, saying they were going to visit the millinery to choose matching bonnets and ribbons.

Elizabeth was unconvinced their actions were innocent.

Where have Lydia and Kitty truly gone? They cannot buy anything until we join them, for they have no money.

While Mrs. Simpson, the modiste, and her assistant measured Jane, Elizabeth stepped to the window, curious to see what her youngest sisters were doing, for she knew Lydia and Kitty usually had a secret plan.

Her curiosity was soon satisfied, though not to her satisfaction. Instead, her cheeks burned in embarrassment.

Lydia and Kitty stood in the street, laughing and talking with several officers, on display for the gossips of Meryton.

Absolutely no sense of propriety. No sense of any sort! Elizabeth frowned as she noticed Lydia had her hand on the arm of George Wickham, looking up at him in blatant adoration.

Fitzwilliam was right to warn me. I shall put an end to this stupidity. She strode from the shop, heading for the merry group. "Kitty, Lydia, you are needed indoors. Come."

Kitty tossed her head but did as she was told, stomping by Elizabeth on her way to the milliner's door.

Lydia assumed a mulish expression and held her ground. "Since I have done all I need to do for the weddings, I feel certain I am not wanted by Mama."

Wickham turned to look at Elizabeth, raising a brow. "Weddings? More than one?"

His eyes are unnaturally bright. The man frightens me, she thought.

"Jane is to marry Mr. Bingley, and Lizzy is to marry Mr. Darcy – in a fortnight," Lydia replied. "Our house is all in uproar, for we found out only today."

Elizabeth groaned inwardly *And now he knows Mr. Darcy shall be your brother. You have made yourself a target with your foolish tendency to tell everything you hear. Indeed, Wickham could have some plan for any or all of us spinning in his head as we speak. He knows 'tis a perfect opportunity to seek revenge on my fiancé.*

Wickham beheld her with open curiosity, his eyes glittering as he dropped Lydia's hand to pull his sleeves down over his thick gloves. "I have known Mr. Darcy all my life. I am quite surprised the gentleman lowered himself to an alliance with a country gentleman's daughter, however lovely you may be, for he moves in the highest circles of society. Your father must be well-connected and wealthy. The proud man of my acquaintance would never marry for less than a fortune, unless the lady descended from a titled family."

Lydia guffawed. "Heavens, no! We have very little in the way of dowries, and our father is not of noble birth."

"Then he made a love match?" He grimaced. "I had no idea he was capable of such tender feelings."

"I can hardly believe it myself," Lydia said, chortling. "He seems so severe. I cannot recall ever seeing Mr. Darcy smile until today."

"You shall cease discussing my betrothed in the public streets," Elizabeth replied with spirit, glaring at her sister, her eyes fiery. "He is the most honourable man of my acquaintance. You hardly know him, though I am certain you will be ready enough to enjoy the benefits of being related to him by marriage."

"Ah, Miss Elizabeth, but I have been acquainted with your *betrothed* for more than twenty-five years, and he has treated me most abominably," said Wickham, laughing unpleasantly as his gaze raked her up and down.

"Dear Wickham was just telling Kitty and me how Mr. Darcy cheated him out of his inheritance when you joined us, Lizzy," added Lydia, pointing at her. "You are the one who has no understanding of the man."

Wickham's smug grin further angered Elizabeth. *He is unbalanced. Why can Lydia not see it?*

"Mr. Wickham told you his version of the story," she said, her face red, "but Mr. Darcy enlightened me as to the true events before he left Longbourn earlier today. In fact, at Mr. Wickham's request, Mr. Darcy gave him £3000 in lieu of the living at Kympton, for he had no desire to be a parson."

Lydia stared at him, covering her mouth with her hand. "Is that true, Mr. Wickham? Did Mr. Darcy pay you?"

His face flushed, betraying his foul temper. "I should have had more than that. Darcy has far more money than he needs," he said angrily.

"But he gave you the amount you asked, did he not?" asked Elizabeth, narrowing her eyes. "He could have given you nothing, but he honoured his father's request."

"I shall not stand here and bear your insults!" he declared with menace, glaring at her. "You shall pay dearly for this." He clenched his fists in their thick leather gloves, then turned on his heel and strode away without a backward glance.

Lydia sighed dramatically. "Such a shame, for he is fearful handsome."

"I do not find him so," Elizabeth answered shortly. "I think he is frightening."

Lydia's wheedling voice grated on her sister's nerves. "He is not so very bad, is he? I can understand that he wished for more money. I would like a fortune, too."

"He lied to all of us," replied Elizabeth in a hard tone. "You know not what a blackguard he is, and I am not at liberty to enlighten you. However, you *will* stay away from the man, for he would ruin our family without a second thought. You heard him threaten me. He is evil."

"You shall not prevent us from talking to Mr. Wickham. He is an officer in the militia, and Mama will allow us to be friends with him," said Lydia, flouncing away in the direction of the milliner's.

Elizabeth hurried back to the dressmaker's shop.

She opened the door and was greatly relieved to see that Jane was finished.

Mrs. Bennet gestured for her second eldest to come to her, fluttering her hands. "Where have you been, Lizzy? 'Tis late in the afternoon. You must hurry to order your dress, for Mrs. Simpson shall soon close her shop, and we must return to Longbourn. I invited the gentlemen to dinner, you know."

Elizabeth nodded, forcing herself to smile. *I shall have to tell Mr. Darcy of Mr. Wickham's intentions.*

"Mama, Lydia and Kitty have gone to select bonnets and ribbons. I feel certain they would benefit from your advice and, and Jane must select hers. You two go join them at the millinery, for they need your help in choosing appropriately. I shall be along directly to select mine."

"Well, you must be quick, then," her mother replied, bustling from the shop, chattering. "We shall be having your fiancé as well as Jane's at Longbourn for dinner this evening, and I need to hurry home to supervise the preparations. Mr. Darcy once complimented me on my skills as a hostess, you know, and I would not have him or Mr. Bingley disappointed. Everything must be perfect for the gentlemen."

Mrs. Simpson greeted Elizabeth. "I am so happy to be entrusted with your wedding gown, my dear. I already have your measurements. Shall I help you choose your fabric and pattern?"

"Thank you, yes," she answered, following the woman to the rear of the building.

Within an hour, the Bennet carriage was travelling the road back to Longbourn.

Darcy and Bingley arrived at Longbourn just before the carriage, so they waved away the footman and helped the ladies themselves.

Once everyone had been assisted in leaving the conveyance, the party approached the front door.

Elizabeth, escorted by Darcy, whispered, "We must talk before you go this evening. I must speak with you on a most serious matter which cannot be delayed until your return."

He nodded. "After dinner then," he replied, inclining his head to speak into her ear.

They soon assembled in the dining room, but it seemed an eternity to Elizabeth before they finished eating and left the room for the parlour.

After an interminable half hour of polite conversation, Darcy caught Bingley's eye.

"We really must take our leave, Mrs. Bennet, for we intend to be off to London before the sun rises," Darcy said.

Mr. Bennet acquiesced. "'Tis growing late. I wish you a pleasant journey."

Shortly afterwards, the two gentlemen expressed their wishes to walk a few moments in the gardens with their fiancées.

Mrs. Bennet smiled and directed a footman to light the torches. "I quite understand your desire for private goodbyes."

Once they were safely away from listening ears, Elizabeth relayed her fears to her betrothed.

Darcy's dark eyes flashed in anger. "The blackguard had the audacity to threaten you and your family? I shall handle this while I am in London. Tell your father about Wickham, for he must insist that your younger sisters remain at home tomorrow. Take care that none of you go anywhere by yourselves. Bingley and I will be gone only a day, for I now comprehend we cannot be away any longer. I will protect what is mine."

He called to Bingley, and the younger man began to walk toward them, smiling at Jane as he escorted her.

"We shall depart earlier than we originally planned in order to be in London by eight o'clock. Therefore, we cannot linger," said Darcy, pulling Elizabeth to him, kissing her gently on her forehead. "I shall write a letter to your father and have it delivered in the morning. Do not be anxious, my love."

She smiled, turning her face up to his. "I shall not worry, for I have confidence in you. Take care. My heart travels with you."

The gentlemen, though expressing their reluctance to leave, escorted their brides safely back to Longbourn before they mounted their horses and rode away.

ROBIN HELM

CHAPTER 23

Finally, brethren, whatever things are true, whatever things are noble, whatever things are just, whatever things are pure, whatever things are lovely, whatever things are of good report, if there is any virtue and if there is anything praiseworthy—meditate on these things.
Philippians 4:8

Darcy and Bingley left for London before the sun rose, intent on completing their business and returning to Netherfield in time to sleep for a few hours and meet their fiancées at daybreak the following morning.

As soon as the light was sufficient to write a schedule, the gentlemen wisely used their time in the carriage to plan their day.

"I must post a letter to Georgiana. She may wish to attend the wedding with my aunt, if they are able to come on such short notice. Then, I have to visit my lawyer to draw up the settlement papers and make changes to my will. I shall provide for Elizabeth as my wife, and for her family in the event that her father should precede her mother in death," said Darcy.

Bingley nodded. "We can do that together, for we use the same man. I must update my will, as well. My sisters shall get what my father promised, but no more. Jane will take precedence now. I plan to do my part to help her mother and younger sisters, too, so you and

I can decide on what is fair, especially in the event that the younger sisters do not marry men of good fortune."

"The dower house at Pemberley will do very well for Mrs. Bennet and any unmarried daughters, if the worst happens, but they shall need also an allowance for their expenses." Darcy wrote in his journal with a pencil he brought along, determined to forget nothing.

He frowned at the page, dissatisfied with his scrawl. "My handwriting looks fully as bad as yours, Bingley."

"Only because of the jolting carriage," Bingley replied, chuckling. "Once we handle the settlements, I shall retrieve the ring my mother left for my wife. My father left it with our banker for safekeeping, for Caroline has had her eye on it for many years now."

Darcy shook his head. "I shall note the visit to the banker, as I have business there, as well. We must stop in at Darcy House, too. Perhaps we might break our fast there while I speak with the housekeeper and butler. I wish for everything to be perfect when Elizabeth and I arrive after the wedding."

"Excellent. While you instruct your staff, I shall do the same with mine. Very fortunate that our houses are so close together."

Darcy bent his head to continue the list. "One of the footmen travelling with the coachman on the carriage can deliver a note to Darcy House concerning our meal while we see the solicitor and banker. I also plan to arrange our wedding trip. Elizabeth has long wanted to travel, and I look forward to making that dream of hers a reality."

"I need to do that, as well. I shall go with you," answered Bingley. His statement was met with Darcy's raised eyebrow.

The younger man laughed. "Have no worries, my friend. I do not wish to share my new wife with you and her sister. We shall not travel with you and Miss Elizabeth."

Darcy smiled, glancing out the window. "She shall no longer be 'Miss Elizabeth,' and as you will be both Mrs. Darcy's brother and mine, you may call her by her given name after we marry. You have reminded me of something else, though. Each sister will need a lady's maid to travel with her. Since all the Bennet sisters share one maid, we must handle that when we go to our London houses."

"I just now realized my sisters will be your sisters in two short weeks. Perhaps Caroline will stop her pursuit of you, since you shall be a married man," Bingley smirked, "though I feel sure she shall be most happy to drop your name into multitudes of conversations with her society friends. At any rate, she is gaining a longed-for relationship with your family, and she must be content with that."

"You are likely right, but be aware that I have no intentions of allowing anyone to disparage my wife, neither to her face nor behind her back. We will not receive anyone who does so. You should relay that information to Caroline and Louisa."

Both men were silent while Darcy continued to write.

"I think you may be forgetting something on that list," said Bingley, once his friend glanced up.

The dark-haired gentleman read back through what he had written. "Ah! You are right. Our premier order of business will be to secure an audience with the Archbishop of Canterbury for our special licenses. We shall stop in Doctors Commons first, for he may have a full morning. 'Tis possible he cannot receive us until the afternoon, and that would affect the remainder of our short time in London."

"Indeed, I hope His Excellency is well and willing to see us today."

"I have no doubt he will grant us an audience," replied Darcy.

"How so?"

"Archbishop Manners-Sutton and my father attended Cambridge together, and they maintained a close friendship until my father passed away. I have heard that he eloped with his wife, though my father and I never spoke of it. I met his son several times, first at Eton and later at Cambridge, though he is three years older than I. Quite an intelligent man. It appears he may achieve an important career in politics, for he is already a member of Parliament."

Bingley scratched his chin. "Interesting about the elopement. If that is so, he is likely sympathetic to those who want to marry without waiting for the banns to be read three times."

Darcy chuckled. "Very true. The sooner I am wed to Elizabeth, the sooner I shall be able to protect her from those who are less scrupulous."

"You think someone would harm Miss Elizabeth? Bodily? Do you suspect anyone in particular?" Bingley's pleasant face wore an unaccustomed scowl.

"George Wickham has joined the militia and is stationed in Meryton."

"Why should Wickham want to hurt any of the Bennets? Surely they are nothing to him."

Darcy sighed. "He wishes to hurt me, and he knows Elizabeth and I are betrothed. I told you some of our conflicts."

"Yes, I know he treated you in an abominable manner, but I had no idea he would be spiteful because you were born wealthy and he was not," answered Bingley. "Your family tried to help him, after all."

"I would rather not share our whole history with anyone else, for someone very dear to me is involved. Allow it to be sufficient for me to say he is a rogue – a scoundrel who preys on unsuspecting women and tradesmen, running up debts he cannot pay before he leaves an area. I told you a year or so ago that Wickham and I grew up together, and we know each other very well. His attack on me was – quite personal. Nearly devastating. He knew exactly what would wound me the most."

Bingley nodded. "'Tis clear why you are in such a hurry to return to Netherfield. I thought you wished to spend more time with your betrothed before the wedding, but now I understand you have more than one reason for haste."

"As do you. He may choose to meddle with Miss Bennet or the younger Bennet sisters rather than risk his very life by making my future wife his target. Both of us must do our best to prevent any attacks against those we love."

"You would kill him?" asked Bingley, shocked.

Darcy spoke calmly. "No, but I would make certain he could never again take advantage of a respectable woman. I would leave him alive, for he would suffer more that way."

"Darcy, you cannot mean you would disable him in some way. You are formidable; however, I have never known you to strike a physical blow to anyone."

The gentleman sighed, stretching his long legs as much as was possible in the confined space. "I suppose you are right. I might want to duel with him or ensure that he could no longer live in debauchery, but I would more likely have him transported to Australia. He would probably do far less harm in a colony of prisoners with relatively few women among the population. Far worse men than Wickham have been sent to Australia, and they would regulate his behaviour by brute force if necessary."

"You could do that?"

"Oh, yes. Colonel Fitzwilliam and I have already spoken of it. My cousin and I would have done it already had it not meant exposing a person we both love to the censure of the world. Wickham will not receive such mercy at our hands once more should he betray us in like manner again."

"Remind me never to cross you or your cousin," said Bingley. "I would rather keep all my fingers, toes, and other assorted body parts."

"You have no need to worry, for you are incapable of the types of evil actions which would push us to such extremes."

Darcy added another item to the list. "I must send a note around to my cousin. He may wish to travel back to Netherfield with us."

"Why?" asked Bingley. "Do you require his help in preparing for the wedding?"

"No. I am well able to handle those details. He must visit Colonel Forster and advise him to be careful of the viper in his bosom. Wickham should not be allowed to victimize the good people of Meryton."

Bingley nodded. "His connection with the military would make him the best one to handle that. Shall we go by the newspaper, as well? I should like to announce my engagement to Jane."

Darcy bent over his paper. "Excellent idea. Let the men of England know that the two elder Bennet sisters are no longer available and, at the same time, give the matchmaking mamas of Society notice that you and I are off the marriage market. We can commission the wedding announcement at the same time and instruct them to print it in a fortnight."

With that, the gentlemen lapsed into contented silence until they saw the city in the distance.

After completing their errands in London to their satisfaction, Darcy and Bingley – weary, cold, and hungry – returned to Darcy House for steaming baths, dinner, and a few hours of sleep before they boarded the carriage again.

Colonel Fitzwilliam joined them there, as he had decided to dine with them, sleep at Darcy House, and travel to Meryton in Darcy's comfortable conveyance rather than ride horseback. To say he was eager to handle the business with Wickham would be a vast understatement.

The return journey to Netherfield was largely silent, as the three men elected to sleep rather than engage in conversation. The hot bricks under their feet and heavy blankets covering them soon had them comfortably warm as they drifted off.

However, as the sky began to lighten, Darcy stirred. "We are nearly to Netherfield," he said, gazing out the window of the vehicle.

The gentleman sat up to tap his friend and nudge his cousin. "Wake up, Richard. We shall be there in a few minutes."

Colonel Fitzwilliam sat up, yawning. "Why are you in such a confounded hurry, Darcy?"

The gentleman ignored him, staring out the window.

Bingley rubbed his eyes. "Our fiancées walk every morning and evening, and we escort them back to within sight of Longbourn. I told the grooms to watch for us and have our horses saddled and ready, for I feared we would be too late to meet them if we walked."

"But they did not know to have a horse for me," replied the colonel. "I had no idea you were so enthralled with your ladies. Can you not wait until we can make a proper morning call?"

"We already missed yesterday morning and last evening, and I have no intention of forgoing my opportunity to see Elizabeth now," muttered Darcy. "You certainly do not have to join us."

"Oh, but I insist. I must meet the paragon who has bewitched the unshakeable Fitzwilliam Darcy," he answered, chuckling. "Why, you have been an absolute bear the entire trip. You must miss your Elizabeth a great deal."

Darcy looked him squarely in the eyes. "'Tis *Miss* Elizabeth to you until we marry, and I feel her absence sorely. Do not raise my ire by flirting with her when you meet."

Colonel Fitzwilliam grinned as he raised his hands in mock surrender.

The carriage drew to a stop before the house, and the gentlemen climbed out to see a groom leading Bingley's horse toward them.

"Where is Xanthos?" asked Darcy.

The young man hung his head. "I couldna saddle him, sir. He nearly bit me."

Darcy strode toward the stables. "Come, Richard," he said over his shoulder to his cousin. "They can saddle a horse for you while I handle Xanthos."

"I shall wait for you, but hurry," called Bingley, swinging up into his saddle to follow them. "The sun is beginning to rise."

Before a quarter hour had passed, the three men were galloping to Oakham Mount.

Dawn broke as they reached the top of the hill.

"Where are they?" Darcy peered at the stretch of land before them.

"Perhaps they did not walk today," answered Richard, covering his yawn with his hand.

Bingley shook his head. "My Jane always takes her morning exercise, and she knew I was coming back from London early to see her."

"Perhaps she has overslept, or she could have a cold," offered the colonel.

"They are not like the pampered ladies of London Society. Follow me," said Darcy, kicking Xanthos to a gallop toward Longbourn.

As soon as he saw the tree, he was certain something was very wrong.

He pointed ahead. "There is no ribbon on that oak. Elizabeth promised to tie one there if they were ever unable to walk. She knew I would worry," he said. "I have a terrible feeling about this. Something has happened to them."

Darcy kicked Xanthos and raced toward the house, the other two men close behind him.

Mrs. Bailey came out the front door and stood on the porch, her frightened expression speaking for her. "Did you not meet Miss Bennet and Miss Elizabeth this morning? My girl was excited to see you, Mr. Darcy."

His eyes widened. "When did they leave?"

"At their normal time, or a few minutes earlier. They were so happy you and Mr. Bingley would be home." She wrung her hands as tears filled her eyes.

"I am Darcy's cousin. What colours were they wearing, if you can remember?" asked Colonel Fitzwilliam.

"Miss Elizabeth wore her red coat, and Miss Jane was in light brown."

Darcy turned his horse. "We shall find them, Mrs. Bailey. Do not sound the alarm yet. Perhaps one of the ladies sprained an ankle. Have no fear. They shall soon be back here."

She nodded, watching as the three men rode away.

CHAPTER 24

*If we say that we have no sin, we deceive ourselves, and the truth is
not in us.*
I John 1:8

"Spread out!" Darcy yelled as they rode. "Look for any sign of a
struggle!"

"I have the right!" shouted Colonel Fitzwilliam. "Darcy to the
left, and Bingley up the center!"

They were midway to Oakham Mount when Darcy spotted a
flash of colour and a few broken branches low to the ground
amongst the trees. "I found something!" he called as he pulled
Xanthos to a halt, flung himself from the horse, and raced to
investigate, knowing the other men would be close behind him.

The sight before him chilled his blood. There, in front of him,
lay Elizabeth's soiled red bonnet, the ribbon torn and dirty, as if it
had been ripped from her head and thrown roughly aside. His heart
aching, he knelt to retrieve it and crushed it to his chest.

Colonel Fitzwilliam spoke quietly from behind him. "What have
you found, Darcy?"

Darcy, grief-stricken, stood and held the bonnet out for his
cousin to see. "This is Elizabeth's. I have seen it many times before."

"She is well, Darcy. There is no blood on it. Cousin, we shall find her," said the colonel firmly. "And whoever did this to your betrothed will certainly pay."

Bingley briefly put his hand on his friend's shoulder, then ran further into the woods. "I see her! There! She is just in front of us!" he cried.

Darcy and the colonel ran toward his voice. *Dear God, let her be unharmed.*

Bingley had his front to them, on his knees, kneeling before a lady who sat tied to a tree. Her hair was hidden under a white bonnet.

Darcy held Elizabeth's red bonnet in his hand, so he knew it was not his fiancée. His head down, he approached the lady and walked to stand in front of her.

Jane did not move, and his heart nearly stopped. *Is she dead?*

She opened her eyes and turned her frightened gaze upward to look up at him. Darcy saw to his relief that she was conscious.

"Jane," moaned Bingley, his hands cupping her face. "Jane, my love. I am here."

"Help me remove the ropes, Darcy," said Colonel Fitzwilliam with authority from behind him. "Bingley, try to untie the gag. She appears to be unharmed, and she needs to tell us where her sister is."

With Darcy's assistance, Jane was quickly freed.

She put her hands over her eyes and began to cry. "He took her," she choked out. "He said she would suffer," she wailed. "He held a gun to her head and forced her to tie me up."

Darcy closed his eyes in an effort to restrain himself. "Who took her? Was it Wickham?" He forced the words out.

Jane put her hands in her lap, nodded, and sobbed afresh. "He said he would come back for me, but he could not handle both of us at once. He said you would no longer want my sister when he is finished with her."

Colonel Fitzwilliam's voice was soft and gentle. "Dry your eyes, Miss Bennet. I promise you, we shall find your sister. All will be well, but we need any help you can give us. Did you see which direction Wickham went?"

"He wrenched her arm behind her back and took her in the direction I was facing. That way," she said, pointing into the forest. "I watched until they were out of sight." The tears rolled down her face while she wrung her hands.

Bingley moved to sit beside Jane as Darcy knelt before her, taking her cold hands in his. "Had he harmed her?" he asked quietly.

Jane nodded. "She cried out when he did that to her arm, and he struck her across her face. Her nose was bleeding." Her voice grew deadly quiet. "I hate him. God help me, I hate him! I have never felt this way about anyone else." She wept into her hands. "How could he do that? My sister has done nothing to him – she does not deserve such treatment. He has taken leave of his senses."

Darcy bowed his head, clenching his jaw. *He did it to get back at me. Had she not agreed to be my wife, she would be safe at home right now. I would gladly pay any amount to have her back unharmed. Dear God, I pray she is not suffering.*

Colonel Fitzwilliam tapped Darcy's shoulder. "We must go now. Perhaps we can find her quickly. Bingley, is there a way for you to get her into Longbourn without being observed? Miss Bennet needs to be in a warm place with something to eat and drink, but I would rather not raise speculation or give way to gossip by apprising her family and the neighbourhood of these events."

Bingley stood and held out his hand to Jane. "Come, dearest. We can take my horse to Longbourn and enter the back way. Your Mrs. Bailey will let us in the servants' entrance."

She took his fingers, allowing him to help her to her feet, her voice cracking as she spoke. "But what of Lizzy? I want to go with the colonel and Mr. Darcy. She will need me."

Her fiancé shook his head. "No, my love. Darcy and Colonel Fitzwilliam will be able to handle the situation better without us along. You are cold. I would not have you become ill, and neither would Miss Elizabeth. Come."

Jane allowed him to lead her to his horse. He swung himself up into the saddle, reached down for Jane, and instructed her to put her foot in the stirrup. Then he helped her settle in front of him, holding her to him with an arm around her waist.

"We shall await you at Longbourn," he said to the other men over his shoulder before they rode away.

Darcy mounted Xanthos and waited for Colonel Fitzwilliam. "North through the woods?"

"Yes. What lies in that direction?"

"I think Meryton first, and then the encampment farther on. Would he have taken her there?"

The colonel laughed bitterly as he leapt onto his horse. "I highly doubt that. No true English soldier would excuse his actions. He will have found some place to keep her hidden. I suspect he must report this morning or face disciplinary action, and he cannot go there with a gentleman's daughter he has kidnapped. She is no tradesman's girl. He could face execution for this. At the very least, transport to Australia."

"I cannot stand to think of her alone, afraid, in pain," Darcy replied, his voice rough, as he led the way through the trees.

Colonel Fitzwilliam rode up beside him, dodging trees while he scanned the ground. "This way. Look at that," he said, pointing to disturbed soil. "She fought him every step. I wonder if she did it to leave a trail for us."

"She is very capable of thinking of that, especially if she is angry rather than frightened," answered Darcy.

"No shrinking violet, then?"

"Not my Elizabeth," he answered. "She once told me that her courage rises with every attempt to intimidate her."

"Good. She likely has need of her bravery," said Colonel Fitzwilliam, stopping short, leaning forward in his saddle. "Look yonder. A hut. What do you know of it?"

"Elizabeth mentioned it once as we were walking, but I have never explored the area very much. It belonged to an old man who lived alone. He watched the land for poachers, and reported them to the former owners of Netherfield, I think. 'Tis now uninhabited, if I remember correctly."

"Then why do I see your betrothed's tracks leading in that direction?" asked the colonel, edging his horse onward.

"She is in there," Darcy replied in low voice.

"Just so. When we draw a little closer, we shall dismount and approach on foot, very quietly. No talking from this point on."

Darcy nodded in agreement.

Soon they were on the edge of the trees surrounding the clearing, the hut in front of them. After they both jumped down and tied their horses to low branches, they bent low and crept closer to peek into a window.

Darcy's heart thudded in his chest.

She lay on the filthy floor, her hands bound behind her, her ankles together, with a dirty cloth stuffed into her mouth. Her eyes were closed, and he could see blood on her face.

He started to stand, but his cousin put out a hand to stop him. Colonel Fitzwilliam pulled a pistol from his coat and gestured for Darcy to follow him.

They circled the small building quietly, keeping close to the ground, looking in each window until they arrived at the door.

"It appears she is alone," the colonel whispered, "but we must be careful. Wickham could be hiding behind the door, waiting for us. He might hurt her even more if sees us and decides to use her for a hostage."

Darcy drew his weapon from a hidden pocket in his greatcoat and cocked it. *I will kill him if he touches her again.*

Colonel Fitzwilliam shook his head. "Let me handle this."

Darcy glared at him, motioning forward.

The colonel sighed, pushing the door. The rusted hinges creaked loudly as it opened a bit.

There was no discernable movement beyond the door, so Colonel Fitzwilliam moved into the room a small distance, remaining mostly hidden.

An explosion shattered the silence, the shot whizzing just to the side of the colonel's head.

Darcy grunted, his left hand flying to the fleshy part of his right shoulder.

The colonel looked behind him at the sound.

This is insanity, even for Wickham. He belongs in Bedlam. "No, Richard. Get Elizabeth!" Darcy shouted. "'Tis but a scratch."

The door flew open, displaying Wickham a few feet away, just out of reach, pointing a double-barrelled pistol at the two of them.

"Yes, *Richard*," he spat, hatred in his eyes. "By all means, come in. While I despoil *Elizabeth*, we shall allow my childhood friend to watch."

The colonel straightened up slowly, cocking his gun, levelling it to aim at Wickham's head. "Have you completely lost your mind? Are you determined on your course, Wickham? You have a weapon, but both of us are armed. You may shoot one of us, but the other will shoot you, and we will shoot to kill. Right now, you are guilty only of kidnapping. Would you increase your sentence by murdering one of us or molesting a gentleman's daughter?"

Wickham hesitated a moment, then quickly turned his pistol toward Elizabeth. Her eyes flew open and widened in fear.

"If you shoot me, I shall shoot her. She will die with me." His eyes were bright with madness, a grotesque smile on his lips.

Darcy stepped around his cousin, firing his gun. As the shot struck Wickham's gloved hand, he dropped his pistol and fell to the floor, moaning over his injury.

Darcy hastened to Elizabeth, untying her, checking for injuries, while Colonel Fitzwilliam strode to Wickham and towered over him. He kicked the weapon out of his reach, kneeling beside the injured man.

"You seem to have forgotten all those times we practiced shooting at Pemberley, you fool. One of us nearly always won. It was never you, and it was seldom me. Darcy was the crack shot. He bested you every time."

Wickham looked up at him, malice in his expression, his voice unnaturally high. "He has very likely ruined my hand."

The colonel chuckled, a threat in the sound. "You are a fortunate man. He could just as easily have put that shot between your eyes. He showed you mercy. I would not have done so. Darcy spared your life by shooting before I did." He leaned over Wickham. "Get up. The colonel of your regiment will be most interested in your activities this day."

Darcy looked up. "No, he cannot go back and tell what he did. Think a moment."

Colonel Fitzwilliam glared at him. "I see your point. Why did you not simply kill him?"

"He spared him because he knew I would see it," answered Elizabeth, standing to her feet with Darcy's help. "Now, he shall spare him again so there is no damage to my reputation, just as he did with his sister."

"Tie him up securely. We shall leave him here while we decide what to do. I must take Elizabeth back to Longbourn. You shall follow us there. We shall talk with Mr. Bennet and lay a course of action."

The colonel nodded, a glum expression on his face. "As usual, Wickham is far more trouble than he is worth. However, I shall have to take him to the encampment to have his hand treated, or he could bleed to death." Colonel Fitzwilliam began to remove his cravat. "I can wrap it to slow the loss of blood."

"He must not be allowed to speak of this. Can you prevent him?" asked Darcy.

The colonel smiled. "I will stay by him. Perhaps I shall make certain he is unconscious when we arrive, though I would rather he felt the pain of having his hand treated."

"Fitzwilliam, your shoulder – the blood," Elizabeth said in obvious distress. She bent over and tore the ruffle from the bottom of her dress. "Hold still while I tie this around the wound."

Darcy allowed her to secure the bandage, knowing she would be upset if he did not allow it.

He frowned. "There is blood on your face, as well." He pulled a handkerchief from his pocket, doing his best to wipe away the stain from under her nose. "Let us go before I change my mind about killing him."

She nodded, and they left the hut, bound for Longbourn while the colonel dealt with Wickham.

CHAPTER 25

"The Spirit of the Lord God is upon Me,
Because the Lord has anointed Me
To preach good tidings to the poor;
He has sent Me to heal the brokenhearted,
And the opening of prison to those who are blind.
To give them beauty for ashes,
The oil of joy for mourning,
The garment of praise for the spirit of heaviness;
That they may be called trees of righteousness,
The planting of the Lord, that He may be glorified."
Isaiah 6:1, 3

Mrs. Bailey was most resourceful, quite successful in concealing the events of the early morning from the rest of the household.

After Mr. Bingley arrived with Jane and told her what had happened, she sent him back to Netherfield and took Jane upstairs, escorting her to the room she shared with Elizabeth. After calling for the maid and sending her straightaway for hot water and towels, she helped Jane to quickly undress, don her nightclothes, wash herself as best she could, and return to bed.

Knowing that Elizabeth would soon follow, Mrs. Bailey hurried back down the stairs to await her at the servants' entrance. Before long, Darcy arrived, holding Elizabeth in front of him on the saddle.

He jumped down, turning to help her dismount, cradling her in his arms to keep her from falling. "Elizabeth, I am sorry, but I must go. Mrs. Bailey will care for you, and I shall return in a few hours. We shall do whatever you want. I have a special license. We can marry today if that is your desire."

She made no reply, though she clung to him.

His expressive eyes spoke his sadness as he looked at Mrs. Bailey. "She is badly hurt. As much as I hate to leave her now, I know that I must. Please, be careful of her arm. It may be out of joint. I dare not call for the local apothecary, but I shall send to London for my physician. Elizabeth is well acquainted with Mr. Beckett, and he knows how to be discrete. I will return at a proper time to call, for I must speak with Mr. Bennet."

Darcy gently set his betrothed on her feet, kissing her cheek tenderly and staying until Mrs. Bailey assured him of her ability to lead Elizabeth indoors.

Within a very short time, Elizabeth was in her room with Jane, allowing Mrs. Bailey to help her undress and wash.

Neither Jane nor Elizabeth made any protest concerning the ministrations of their housekeeper. Mrs. Bailey clucked her tongue at the bruises which had already begun to form on the sisters. Their ankles and wrists showed the signs of being bound, and Elizabeth's face bore the marks Wickham had inflicted when he hit her. She flinched as Mrs. Bailey attempted to wash all the blood from the scratches and the blow she had suffered to her nose, but she said nothing as silent tears streaked her cheeks.

"There now, my dear," said Mrs. Bailey as she made a sling for Elizabeth's arm. "I shall prop you on pillows and arrange your arm so it does not give you pain. If Mr. Darcy sends an express to London this morning, the physician may be here by this evening."

Fortunately, Mrs. Bennet and her younger daughters had not yet made an appearance, for the state of the elder sisters' clothing and hair upon their arrivals could not have withstood close inspection. The dishevelment and dirt would certainly have led to questions.

"You shall both remain in this room today," she said firmly. "You ladies have been through a terrible ordeal, and I shall tell your mother you are ill, for 'tis the truth. I fear you may be truly sick if you do not rest, and you are to be wed soon. There will be no walking this evening or tomorrow morning."

When neither young woman argued with her, she continued. "I must go see to breakfast, for your parents and sisters will be down soon. Try to sleep, my darlings. I shall bring up tea and hot porridge for you both as soon as Cook has no further need for my help. You are chilled to the bone."

She built up the fire before she left the room. "Penny must come with warming pans for the bed. Your feet are too cold."

When she brought food to them a half hour later, the sisters were fast asleep. She set the tray on the table by the bed, and then hurried back down the stairs.

Darcy rode from Longbourn to the encampment, grimly anticipating speaking with Colonel Forster.

His cousin, Colonel Fitzwilliam stood just outside a large tent. Darcy joined him.

"Where is Wickham? Did you kill him?"

"There was no need to kill the man. He is in this tent with the other afflicted soldiers. I fear he will not live long. Should he speak, no one would believe him. He is mad as a hatter, talking out of his head."

"What do you mean?" Darcy opened the tent flap and strode in, stopping as the sight before him struck him dumb.

A cursory glance informed him there were at least five other solders within, and Mr. Jones, the local apothecary, was going from one bed to the next, examining each of them.

Colonel Fitzwilliam spoke from behind him. "I brought him to the tent to be treated for the damage to his hand, fully intending to leave him here while I spoke with the colonel of this regiment. Mr. Jones was already here, having been called in before the sun came up. He looked at Wickham's bloody hand and told me to remove his coat and shirt to provide him with ease in treating his injury. When I did, the apothecary and I saw the evidence."

Darcy's eyes flashed. "What evidence?"

"Come with me. Mr. Jones is still looking at him."

The men joined the apothecary by Wickham's cot. He appeared to be asleep.

Mr. Jones was shaking his head. "His body is covered with a rash, several sores, and a great many abscesses. He has a fever. I have never met the man until today. You seem to know him. Has he lost weight? Does his hair seem thinner than it was?"

Darcy looked at Wickham critically. "He is leaner than the last time I saw him, and I now notice a bald spot on the crown of his head."

"Mr. Wickham," said the apothecary.

The patient opened his eyes, staring vacantly.

"Is your throat sore? Does your head hurt?" Mr. Jones asked.

"Everything hurts," croaked Wickham. "I am tired. Always tired."

"How long have you had these sores?" Mr. Jones continued, pointing to several ugly spots on his body.

"A year or two, but they do not bother me. My bones and muscles hurt."

"The sores do not hurt?" Mr. Jones's expression was concerned.

Wickham shook his head, trying to sit up. "They never have, but they are unsightly. Just do something for my hand. I wish to put on my shirt and go to the officers' tent for breakfast."

"I fear that will not be possible," answered Mr. Jones, pushing him back down. "You must remain in here with the other men. You are very likely contagious." He proceeded to clean and bandage Wickham's injury, ignoring the patient's loud cursing, and then gestured to Colonel Fitzwilliam and Darcy to join him outside the tent.

The gentlemen followed him.

"What illness does he have?" asked Darcy.

"I have seen it many times," he replied, lowering his voice to a whisper. "The French disease, the great pox. An advanced case. The man has had the disease for several years now. I cannot imagine he did not know what it was, as it is common."

Colonel Fitzwilliam cocked a brow. "Is he healthy enough for a sea voyage?"

The apothecary shook his head. "I fear he would not survive a voyage of weeks or even days. I expect he shall succumb to the disease before long. He was ranting nonsense when you brought him here. In the final stages of this condition, the mind is often affected."

Darcy was quiet for a moment. "Is there nothing you can do for him?"

Mr. Jones shook his head. "There is no cure for this. Not even any medicine to help the afflicted to bear it. Some try mercury, but it does more harm than good. If he is your friend, tell him goodbye now while he still breathes."

Colonel Fitzwilliam crossed his arms. "He was a childhood friend of ours, but no longer. It seems his life of debauchery has finally caught up with him. If he dies, we shall bury him here in Hertfordshire. Wickham has no family left."

"How did his hand come to be in such a state? I had quite a difficult time removing his glove. In fact, I had to cut the leather away. The wound looks very much like it was caused by a gun," added the apothecary, eyeing the gentlemen.

The colonel shook his head. "I cannot tell you. Do you think he was cleaning his gun and it accidentally went off? I found him on the way to Oakham Mount and brought him here."

Mr. Jones looked from one man to the other. "Perhaps. I suppose no one will ever know for certain."

"Be sure your sins will find you out," Darcy muttered as he walked away.

Mr. Darcy, Colonel Fitzwilliam, and Mr. Bingley, having changed clothes and eaten, rode back to Longbourn to speak with Mr. Bennet.

The gentlemen waited in the hallway while Mrs. Bailey went to the library door to announce their arrival, and they heard him tell Mrs. Bailey to show them in.

Darcy introduced Colonel Fitzwilliam to Mr. Bennet, and then took his place by a window. The colonel and Mr. Bingley sat in the two chairs in front of the gentleman's desk.

"You are early this morning," said Mr. Bennet, looking from one solemn face to the other. "To what do I owe the pleasure of your company?"

Darcy walked back to face him. "There is no easy way to say this, sir, so prepare yourself. Your two eldest daughters were attacked by Mr. Wickham this morning while they were walking. Fortunately, we three found them before the ladies suffered permanent injury. They are both safely upstairs in their room now, though I feel sure they will require several days to recuperate." He looked away, taking a deep breath.

After a moment, he continued, returning his gaze to Mr. Bennet. "Miss Elizabeth, particularly, will have bruises and discomfort. I must beg you to keep this information to yourself. Though I would happily marry her today, she may not wish for our plans to change. There will be speculation if we move our wedding date up. I leave it completely to you and your daughters, for Bingley and I have talked. We are both at your disposal."

Mr. Bennet stood to face him. "Mrs. Bailey told me they are ill. Why was I not consulted immediately?"

Colonel Fitzwilliam spoke. "I took custody of Wickham after Darcy shot his hand. He was my prisoner until I handed him over to his regiment. Because of the wound from the gun shot, I took him to the apothecary's tent. However, Mr. Jones was much more concerned about Wickham's disease than he was his wound."

"His disease? Is he contagious? Are my daughters well? What illness does the blackguard have?" the elder gentleman asked, alarmed.

"Your daughters could not have caught the illness," answered Darcy. "He is dying from the French disease as we speak. Wickham tied your daughters, and he struck Elizabeth, but he did not molest them in any other way. Mr. Jones says he is in the final stage of the illness. He can no longer hurt anyone."

Mr. Bennet sat down, lowering his eyes to the top of his desk. "You told me in your letter to forbid my younger daughters to leave the house, but none of us thought to keep the two elder sequestered. Their good sense was supposed to be enough to protect them. How did you not know of the danger to them?"

Darcy put his hand on the older man's shoulder. "He led a debauched life, but he had never attacked anyone. He never tried to force a woman to go anywhere or do anything with him against her will. Wickham always used his abundant charm, and I thought Miss Bennet and Miss Elizabeth would be safe from that. They knew what he was. You must know if I had thought there had been any chance of him hurting the woman I love more than my own life, I would have told you that he was a danger to her. Mr. Jones questions his sanity, as do I."

"Yes, I think you would have warned me," he answered, rubbing his temples with his fingers. "I need to talk with my daughters. Come back this evening, and we shall discuss this further. My inclination is to leave everything as planned, but if they wish to marry earlier, I shall agree to whatever they ask."

"Mr. Beckett should be here from London by then. If you agree, he shall examine my betrothed's arm. When she fought Wickham, he used her roughly, and I fear her arm may be dislocated," said Darcy.

Mr. Bennet wiped his eyes. His words were choked. "My Lizzy struggled with him? I am not surprised. I am glad you shot him. I only wonder that you did not kill him. Go now."

The gentlemen, along with Thaddeus Beckett, returned to Longbourn that evening. Mr. Beckett, accompanied by Mrs. Bailey, went directly to examine his patients, and the other three men were ushered immediately into Mr. Bennet's library.

Mr. Bennet looked up at them, gesturing toward the chairs in front of his desk. "Please, sit down. This shall not take long, and my wife insists that you all stay to dine. Though I know it will be difficult for you to pretend my Jane and Elizabeth are simply confined with colds, it will do much to allay any suspicion on her part."

"They have not left their rooms?" asked Darcy, as soon as he was seated.

"They have not, nor will they until their bruises fade," said Mr. Bennet. "My daughters hope you will understand, but they do not wish to wed earlier than was originally planned. They know their mother would argue with such a change to her plans. Besides, they want to have as much time to heal as is possible."

"May we see them?" asked Mr. Bingley anxiously. "I just want to know Miss Bennet is well."

"Then you shall have to take my word for it," said the elder gentleman with firmness. "They do not wish for you to see them until they heal. The discolouration grows worse with every hour, and Elizabeth's shoulder pains her greatly. Perhaps Mr. Beckett can help her."

Colonel Fitzwilliam leaned forward in his chair. "Beckett examined Wickham before we came here, and he agrees with Mr. Jones. Wickham will likely not survive the next two weeks. I had him moved to a private tent, so he shall have no one to talk to."

"Thank you for that," answered Mr. Bennet. "And thank you for all you did for my daughters."

"They were walking to meet us," said Darcy, barely keeping his composure. "If not for that, they may have stayed safely at home."

"'Tis not your fault." Mr. Bennet looked at him with sympathy. "Lizzy told me a good while ago you met her each morning and evening. She keeps very few secrets from me. I knew it all along, and I was glad of it, for I always feared something might happen to them. And as the girls were together, neither you nor they did anything improper. They would have walked with you or without you. Jane had been taking her exercise alone for many years 'til Lizzy joined her."

"Very kind of you to say so, but I do not think I protected her well enough. I promise to do better after we wed." Darcy stood. "I should like to speak to Beckett once he completes his examination. Otherwise, I shall have to wait until after dinner to hear news of her condition, and I cannot bear it."

Mr. Bingley nodded in agreement. "Please."

"If you remain in here, I will send for the physician. He can tell all of us at once," replied Mr. Bennet.

Darcy nodded, and Mr. Bennet quickly scribbled a note and sent for his manservant.

Within a few moments, Mr. Beckett walked through the door. "Both ladies should be well enough in time for their weddings, if they rest between now and then. Miss Elizabeth's shoulder is sprained, but not dislocated. I have bound it to her side to prevent her from moving it. I shall return tomorrow, and if she is better, I shall fashion a sling to allow her a bit more freedom. Provided she follows my instructions, her shoulder should be significantly stronger and less painful in a week.

"Both she and Miss Bennet have bruising and swelling, but no permanent damage. The swelling will go down quickly, but the bruising will be worse before it is better. By the time of the wedding, it should be mostly faded away. Most of it will be hidden under long sleeves. They may need longer gloves to cover their hands and wrists," he finished, directing his gaze to the floor.

The room was quiet with the knowledge of what the young women had suffered.

Darcy stared at his clenched fists, speaking hesitantly. "What of her face? It was already turning blue and purple when we arrived here this morning. She shall be most distressed if she views herself in a mirror."

"I have no comfort for you, sir," answered Beckett, turning his head to look back at him. "Her nose and cheek are swollen, and the colour darkens by the hour. It will be much better, but not completely healed in time for the ceremony. I have directed Mrs. Bailey to use cold compresses until the pain and welts are gone, but Miss Elizabeth has very fair skin. The bruises will certainly show, but they will be faint."

"Perhaps we should postpone our nuptials. She will want to look her best. I must think of her and not myself," Darcy said unhappily.

Mr. Bennet shook his head. "I know my daughters, and they will not put off the wedding. Lizzy and Jane will find a way to make it right. They will think of something."

He leaned toward Darcy, speaking softly. "You did your best. Elizabeth herself told me the damage was done before you arrived. She does not blame you at all, and she would be quite saddened to hear you claiming the guilt in this situation." He sighed as he stood. "Meanwhile, it is time for dinner. Do your best to have a pleasant countenance, gentlemen. Shall we go?"

He left the room, and the men followed after him.

CHAPTER 26

*Therefore, a man shall leave his father and mother and be
joined to his wife, and they shall become one flesh.*
Genesis 2:24

I can stand it no longer.

After a week without seeing Elizabeth, Darcy was morose. He
had sent her daily gifts – several books, bouquets from Netherfield's
hothouse, sweets, a lovely necklace, gloves, and letters – but not
being able to chart her progress or speak with her himself left him
imagining the worst.

Though she had written short notes thanking him for his kind
attention, she had not commented on her appearance or suffering.
She did not mention her eagerness for their impending nuptials.

Darcy had written of his love for her, but she had not returned
those sentiments.

He feared she held him responsible for her present condition,
and he was distraught. *Is she in terrible pain? Is she angry with me?*
Does she regret her decision to wed? Does she no longer love me?

It ate at Darcy that Beckett saw her every day, and he did not.
As much as it wounded him to think it, if she had decided against
him and in Beckett's favour, he would withdraw his suit.

A few hours after daybreak, he saddled Xanthos himself and
rode to Longbourn where he tied Xanthos to a tree and knocked on

the door. Mrs. Bailey greeted him cordially, receiving the sealed letter he gave her, promising to deliver it to Elizabeth at once.

He hurried around the house to stand under her window and wait, putting his hands behind his back, gripping them together to hide his agitation.

Soon, he was rewarded, for Elizabeth came to the window and opened it. "Good morning, Fitzwilliam. Whatever is the matter? Your letter quite confused me." Her voice floated down to him, soft and sweet.

The tension in his chest eased. "I miss you, of course. I wanted to see you to assure myself that you are well."

She put her hand to the bruise on her face. "I feel better each day, though I know I must be unsightly. Mrs. Bailey has hidden all the mirrors, so I must look terrible."

"Not at all. You are beautiful, as always. Are you in much pain?" He tried to smile, but his feelings were too strong to overcome. As he had never been a very emotional man, dealing with such agitation was foreign to him.

Elizabeth tilted her head. "It lessens each day. I am determined to find a looking glass of some sort today, even if I have to visit my mother's room. We shall wed in a week, and I must know how to prepare."

He glanced at the ground. "Do you still wish to marry me?"

She raised both eyebrows. "Why would I not?"

"I failed to keep you safe."

Her mouth fell open. "Fitzwilliam Darcy! Tell me not that you are shouldering the blame for what he did. Or have you changed your own mind about marrying me?"

He raised his face to hers. "I love you with all my heart, Elizabeth. I told you so many times in my letters, but you have not written that in response. Do you still love me? Even a little? If your affections have changed, I shall remain silent on the subject forevermore."

Darcy thought Elizabeth's eyes turned stormy, but he could not see her very well. He did, however, understand her words.

"I cannot write my feelings for you. My vocabulary is insufficient to describe them. This is the first day I have been allowed out of my bed, and I was most happy to see you until you started spouting nonsense. What is this really about? Why would my affections change in the course of a week when I have not so much as left my chamber? Do you think I am some foolish young girl like my fifteen-year-old sister?"

She paused, understanding dawning on her face. "Or are you perhaps worried about the company I keep while I remain confined to my room?"

"You cared for him a great deal only a short while ago. He was my rival for your hand." Darcy blushed from his neck to the roots of his hair. "Beckett takes care of you while I am forbidden to see you. He is handsomer than I, wealthy, easy in company, and bears the title of Lord Thaddeus. Everyone who knows him, likes him. He is universally admired, and I believe he still holds you in extremely high regard."

She quickly turned from the window and disappeared from his view.

He waited, growing increasingly anxious, until Mrs. Bailey approached him from the back of the house. "Follow me," she said tersely, turning to walk to the servants' entrance.

She opened the door and led him into her small office where Elizabeth sat at the desk, a frown on her face.

He heard the sound of a whisper behind him before the door closed. "Tread lightly."

"Sit," Elizabeth said succinctly.

"Are you angry? With me?" he asked with trepidation. *What have I done?*

She drew her brows together. "You can ask me that? What do you think? Sit."

Darcy was truly puzzled, but he did as she said, sitting across from her, the desk between them. "Why are you angry?"

"You imply that I am flighty, vindictive, inconstant, silly, shallow, and materialistic, yet you ask why am I angry?"

He was appalled. "I neither said nor thought any such things. I said you are beautiful, and I love you."

"How can you love me yet have such an ill opinion of me? And kindly remember 'twas you who sent for Thaddeus. I did not."

Darcy did not see the swollen nose, the dark shadows on her face, the scratches on her cheeks, nor the deep bruising under her eyes. He saw his beloved, lovely, lively Elizabeth with pain in her gaze, not because of physical wounds, not caused by Wickham's attack, but brought into being by his words.

He thought for a moment before he stood up, rounded the desk, and lowered himself until his face was even with hers.

"I am amazed every day that you love me, Elizabeth, for I do not feel worthy of your love. Can you forgive me for doubting you, even for a moment?" He leaned toward her slowly, giving her the opportunity to pull away. She did not, so he kissed her carefully, tenderly.

When he pulled back, he was relieved to the point of dizziness to see her smiling.

"Then you will still marry me in a week, fool that I am?" he asked. *Please, say you will.*

"If I change my mind, I promise you shall be the first to know," she answered. "Thaddeus warned me that my face will not be back to normal by then. Under those circumstances, are you certain you still wish to marry *me* in a week? If we change the date now, there shall not be as much gossip. Everyone in Meryton knows Jane and I have been ill."

"I would marry you today. Shall we call for the parson?"

She chuckled. "My mother has not yet seen my face. Do you really want to do that now?"

"I have thought of something, but I have no wish to have another misunderstanding with you. My idea comes from a desire to make your wedding day happier. I want nothing to mar it for you. This is not for me, for I think you are lovely."

Elizabeth tilted her head. "How could you improve my looks?"

"Beckett told us that you would still have significant and noticeable bruising on our wedding day. I sent you longer gloves to cover your wrists, but I think I know a way to help cover the marks on your face."

"I wondered about the gloves. Thank you, my love. Tell me your idea. I should like to hear what you have to say."

He took a deep breath. "I know you never use rouge or anything to enhance your skin, for you have never needed it. Your complexion is perfect, fair and unblemished."

"Yes?" she encouraged, biting her lip as her eyes danced in merriment.

"If you are uncomfortable with the idea of people noticing your bruises, perhaps powder would help cover them. I have even heard of a powder which incorporates crushed pearls. What is your opinion?" He watched her carefully.

Elizabeth still wore a sling, but she lifted her free hand to his face. "You dear, sweet man. Your suggestion is wonderful."

He lowered his head and looked up at her through his dark lashes. "Excellent news, for I ordered several kinds from London, and they arrived this morning, along with a lotion my aunt uses." He stood up, reached into the pocket of his greatcoat, and produced a parcel. "I thought you might want to experiment a bit."

She rose from the chair and accepted the package. "I appreciate this more than you know. Now I need to return to my room before I am found out. Perhaps you could go 'round to the front door and knock? Your morning visit could distract my mother and sisters while I sneak back up the stairs?"

His expression of horror made her laugh. "I know the sacrifice I am asking of you, my love," she said, "but a quarter hour will be sufficient. Then you may go back to Netherfield and be satisfied with an hour well-spent."

Darcy managed a smile. "I shall be pleased to assist you in any way I can." He kissed her quickly. "Into the fray!"

Her plan worked very well. Within fifteen minutes, she was back in her room undetected, and he was riding Xanthos, leaving Longbourn for Netherfield.

Darcy continued to send his beloved gifts and letters each day and was quite pleased to receive notes bearing the three words he most desired to hear in return. He was encouraged to think he might learn to navigate the treacherous waters of love very well given time.

After Bingley found him saddling Xanthos one morning, the younger man was Darcy's constant companion, visiting Longbourn with him to wave at their fiancées from under their chamber window.

Elizabeth rose early the last day she was to bear the name "Bennet." She looked out her window, laughing as she beheld dark skies and snow falling thick and fast.

Perhaps I shall not look so very odd after all.

Her mother and younger sisters had been allowed in the room to see her and Jane many times in the past week, but she had always managed to be in her bed, covers drawn up to her eyes, feigning sleep or a chill to hide her face.

Jane had handled them all most brilliantly, attending meals for the past few days, offering a few comments regarding Elizabeth's slow recovery while Mr. Bennet winked at her over his newspaper, and Mrs. Bennet chattered about the wedding details.

Today, Elizabeth knew they would see her, and she hoped her plans were good enough to fool them. She had been using a mirror, practicing applying Warren's Milk of Roses under the various powders supplied by her betrothed for several days, and she was rather pleased with the results.

Otherwise, I shall simply pretend to fall on my face, and that would not be likely to convince anyone, given that my bruises are not fresh.

Fitzwilliam will marry me either way. If people notice my fading bruises, it shall not matter. My husband and I will be gone, and the gossip will soon die down. Nothing can spoil this day for me.

Jane spoke from beside her. "The higher neckline and collar of your pelisse will seem wise rather than odd, and our choice of head coverings shall not be questioned. No one will see your shoulder, as long as you wear that lovely coat. Your bruises are nearly gone, in any case. When you wear the lotion and powder, they are barely noticeable."

Elizabeth laughed. "If anyone braves the snow to attend the wedding, it will be a great surprise. The four of us may end up standing before the parson in his parlour."

"And should it be in the church, 'tis so dark, no one will see your face clearly. Candles would make even more shadows. Would you like some toast to tide you over until the wedding breakfast? I think we must eat something."

Smiling impishly, Elizabeth replied, "Toast? No, today I want a cookie. Possibly two."

She stood beside her groom before the altar of the church, a delicate lace veil over her bonnet, concealing her face to her chin, and her coat covering her from her chin to the floor. Jane, also wearing a coat and veil, was by Darcy, and Bingley was to her left.

Only the families and a few close friends of the bridal party were in attendance, as the weather had not improved, but instead seemed to worsen by the hour.

"We shall not stay long at the breakfast, my lovely Mrs. Darcy, if that suits you. The snow is getting heavier by the minute, and I should not like for us to be stranded in the cold," Darcy whispered to his bride at the conclusion of the ceremony. He took her arm, carefully helping her into the carriage for the short ride from the church to Longbourn.

She smiled up at him as he sat beside her, nodding in agreement. "Mrs. Darcy. How well that sounds. I quite like it. And the sooner we depart, the less need there will be for me to remove my coat and bonnet."

"I fear we shall not make it to London today, my love," he added. "Shall we spend our wedding night at Netherfield?"

"Will that not expose me further to Charles's sisters?"

Darcy chuckled. "Beckett and I have made a plan. I think it shall be quite effective."

"You and Thaddeus have agreed upon a course of action? Together? Marvelous. Do tell me of this plot."

"You shall soon see for yourself," he replied, smiling as he lifted her veil a bit to kiss her, carefully angling his head to avoid hitting her poor nose.

She had no further opportunity to question him, for he took full advantage of their few moments alone.

Once they had greeted everyone, Mrs. Bailey handed Darcy a basket. "I packed some of Elizabeth's favourite foods for your trip."

"Cookies?" he asked, eyes twinkling.

"Of course," she answered. "Shall you still love her if she eats a few and gains a bit of weight?"

He grinned. "Rest easy, Mrs. Bailey. I shall adore Elizabeth always, through thick or thin. If she should increase, that shall simply be more for me to love."

She patted his arm. "You might just deserve her. Get along with you then. The snow is falling harder."

He handed the basket to a footman, instructing him to place it in his carriage, then found his bride standing with the newly married Bingleys and offered her his arm.

Elizabeth never had to deal with impertinent questions or inquiring glances as they circled the room, greeting their guests, and the reason was obvious.

Thaddeus Beckett at his most charming proved to be quite invaluable in distracting Caroline Bingley and the younger Bennet sisters at the wedding breakfast, and his aid continued once they all arrived at Netherfield.

Caroline never so much as glanced at Elizabeth.

Elizabeth quite aptly said, once she was alone with Darcy in their room, "Your plan worked brilliantly, my love, for how could she look away from Apollo at his most charming?"

"You managed to do so, so I suppose it can be done," answered her husband, pulling her into his embrace to kiss her.

She stood on her tiptoes, whispering in his ear, "Only because even Apollo's charm dims in the presence of Heracles, the one who surpassed all other mortal men."

He kissed her, then leaned back a bit to look at her. "So, you prefer a half-mortal man to a god?"

"A demigod of superhuman strength, violent passions, and unmatched bravery, who is the epitome of masculinity? My own protector?" she asked. "I would be a fool, indeed, to trade the love of such a paragon for a mere god."

Darcy smiled. "If I am very fortunate, you will always feel that way."

"Then, consider yourself a blessed man, and kiss me again, my husband." She put her hands behind his neck, encouraging him.

He did as she ordered, for though he had formidable might and power, he never could resist the call of his own personal siren.

The End

The sequel to *More to Love*: *My Beloved, My Friend (Book 1)*
is *I Dream of You* by Robin Helm, included in
A Very Austen Valentine: Austen Anthologies, Book 2.
https://www.amazon.com/gp/product/B07L6SR1RJ/

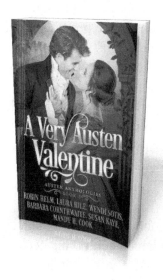

The author will also publish a standalone of
I Dream of You: My Beloved, My Friend (Book 2)

The third book in the series is *Maestro*, scheduled for release
in November 2019.

ABOUT THE AUTHOR

Robin Helm's books reflect her love of music, as well as her fascination with the paranormal and science fiction.

Previously published works include The Guardian Trilogy: *Guardian*, *SoulFire*, and *Legacy*; the Yours by Design series: *Accidentally Yours*, *Sincerely Yours*, and *Forever Yours*; and *Understanding Elizabeth* (Regency romance).

She plans to publish *Maestro*, *Lawfully Innocent*, and *A Very Austen Romance: Austen Anthologies, Book 3* in 2019.

She lives in sunny South Carolina and adores her one husband, two married daughters, and three grandchildren.

Follow her Amazon Author Page for information concerning her new releases.

https://www.amazon.com/Robin-Helm/e/B005MLFMTG/

If you liked *More to Love*, Robin recommends:

https://www.amazon.com/Wendi-Sotis/e/B005CSBVFS/

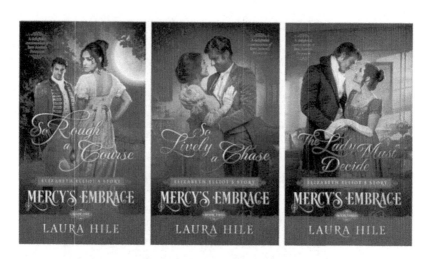

https://www.amazon.com/Laura-Hile/e/B003UT6VDS/

If you enjoyed reading *More to Love*, please join the Christian Indie Authors Readers Group on Facebook. You will find Christian books in multiple genres, opportunities to find other Christian authors, and learn about new releases, sales, and free books. Just type Christian Indie Authors Readers Group into the search bar on Facebook and join us:

https://www.facebook.com/groups/291215317668431/

Made in the USA
Columbia, SC
16 February 2019